THE TATTOO.

"I, too!" Drioli was shouting. "I, too, have a picture by this painter! He was my friend and I have a picture which he gave to me!"

"There!" he cried, breathing quickly. "You see? There it is!"

There was a sudden absolute silence in the room, each person arrested in what he was doing, standing motionless in a kind of shocked, uneasy bewilderment. They were staring at the tattooed picture. It was still there, the colors as bright as ever, but the old man's back was thinner now, the shoulder blades protruded more sharply, and the effect, though not great, was to give the picture a curiously wrinkled, squashed appearance.

The gallery owner was pushing through the crowd towards Drioli. "Monsieur," he said, "I will buy it. I said I would buy it, Monsieur."

Drioli opened his mouth to speak. No words came, so he shut it; then he opened it again and said slowly, "But how can I sell it?"

"Listen," the dealer said, coming up close. "I will help you, I will make you rich. Together we shall make some private arrangement over this picture, no?"

—from "Skin"

Books by Roald Dahl

Speak
Published by Penguin Group
Penguin Group (USA) Inc.,
345 Hudson Street, New York, New York 10014, U.S.A.
Penguin Books Ltd, 80 Strand, London WC2R ORL, England
Penguin Books Australia Ltd, 250 Camberwell Road, Camberwell, Victoria 3124, Australia
Penguin Books Canada Ltd, 10 Alcorn Avenue, Toronto, Ontario, Canada M4V 3B2
Penguin Books (N.Z.) Ltd, 182-190 Wairau Road, Auckland 10, New Zealand

First published in Great Britain by Puffin Books, 2000
First published in the United States of America by Viking,
a division of Penguin Putnam Books for Young Readers, 2000
Published by Puffin Books,
a division of Penguin Putnam Books for Young Readers, 2002
This edition published by Speak, an imprint of Penguin Group (USA) Inc., 2003

7   9   10   8

"Skin," "Lamb to the Slaughter," "The Sound Machine," "Galloping Foxley,"
"The Wish," "Dip in the Pool," and "My Lady Love, My Dove" appeared
in *Someone Like You*, published in the United States of America by
Alfred A. Knopf, Inc., 1953, and in Great Britain by Secker & Warburg Ltd., 1954,
copyright © Roald Dahl, 1953; revised, expanded edition published in Great Britain
by Michael Joseph Ltd, 1961, copyright © Roald Dahl, 1961.

"An African Story" and "Beware of the Dog" appeared in *Over to You* published in Great
Britain by Hamish Hamilton Ltd., 1946, and in the United States of America by Reynal &
Hitchcock, 1946. Copyright © Roald Dahl, 1946.

"The Surgeon" appeared in *Playboy*, 1986. Copyright © Roald Dahl, 1986.

"The Champion of the World" appeared in *Kiss Kiss*, published in Great Britain by Michael
Joseph Ltd., 1959, and in the United States of America by Alfred A. Knopf, Inc., 1960.
Copyright © Roald Dahl, 1959.

THE LIBRARY OF CONGRESS HAS CATALOGED THE VIKING EDITION AS FOLLOWS:
Dahl, Roald.
Skin and other stories / Roald Dahl.
p. cm.
Contents: Skin—Lamb to the slaughter—The sound machine—An African story—Galloping
Foxley—The wish—The surgeon—Dip in the pool—The champion of the world—
Beware of the dog—My lady love, my dove.
Summary: Introduces teenagers to the adult short stories of Roald Dahl
ISBN: 0-670-89184-3 (hc)
1. Short stories, English. [1. Short stories.] I. Title.
PZ7.D1515 Sk 2000 [fic]—dc21 99-058600 CIP

This edition ISBN 0-14-131034-0

Printed in the United States of America

Roald Da

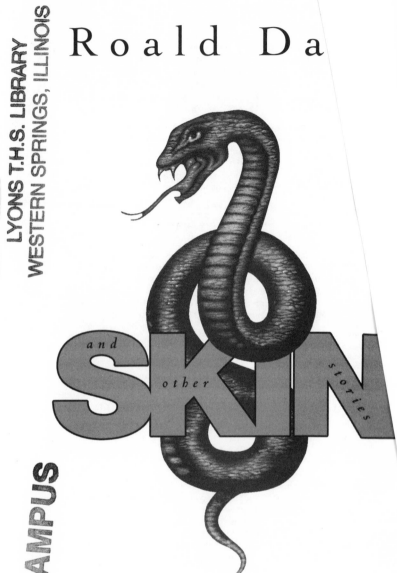

and S*other* KI*stories*N

speak
An Imprint of Penguin Group (USA) Inc.

and other stories

CONTENTS

SKIN

That year—1946—winter was a long time going. Although it was April, a freezing wind blew through the streets of the city, and overhead the snow clouds moved across the sky.

The old man who was called Drioli shuffled painfully along the sidewalk of the rue de Rivoli. He was cold and miserable, huddled up like a hedgehog in a filthy black coat, only his eyes and the top of his head visible above the turned-up collar.

The door of a café opened and the faint whiff of roasting chicken brought a pain of yearning to the top of his stomach. He moved on glancing without any interest at the things in the shop windows—perfume, silk ties and shirts, diamonds, porcelain, antique furniture, finely bound books. Then a picture gallery. He had always liked picture galleries. This one had a single canvas on display in the window. He stopped to look at it. He turned to go on. He checked, looked back; and now, suddenly, there came to him a slight uneasiness, a movement of the memory, a distant recollection of something, somewhere, he had seen before. He looked again. It was a landscape, a clump of trees leaning madly over to one side as if blown by a tremendous wind, the sky swirling and twisting all around. Attached to the frame there was a little plaque, and on this it said: CHAÏM SOUTINE (1894–1943).

Drioli stared at the picture, wondering vaguely what there was about it that seemed familiar. Crazy painting, he thought. Very strange and crazy—but I like it . . . Chaïm Soutine . . . Soutine . . . "By God!" he cried suddenly. "My little Kalmuck, that's who it is! My little Kalmuck with a picture in the finest shop in Paris! Just imagine that!"

The old man pressed his face closer to the window. He could remember the boy—yes, quite clearly he could remember him. But when? The rest of it was not so easy to recollect. It was so long ago. How long? Twenty—no, more like thirty years, wasn't it? Wait a minute. Yes—it was the year before the war, the first war, 1913. That was it. And this Soutine, this ugly little Kalmuck, a sullen brooding boy whom he had liked—almost loved—for no reason at all that he could think of except that he could paint.

And how he could paint! It was coming back more clearly now—the street, the line of refuse cans along the length of it, the rotten smell, the brown cats walking delicately over the refuse, and then the women, moist fat women sitting on the doorsteps with their feet upon the cobblestones of the street. Which street? Where was it the boy had lived?

The Cité Falguière, that was it! The old man nodded his head several times, pleased to have remembered the name. Then there was the studio with the single chair in it, and the filthy red couch that the boy had used for sleeping; the drunken parties, the cheap white wine, the furious quarrels, and always, always the bitter sullen face of the boy brooding over his work.

It was odd, Drioli thought, how easily it all came back to him now, how each single small remembered fact seemed instantly to remind him of another.

There was that nonsense with the tattoo, for instance. Now, *that* was a mad thing if ever there was one. How had it started? Ah, yes—he had got rich one day, that was it, and he had bought lots of wine. He could see himself now as he entered the studio with the parcel of bottles under his arm—the boy sitting before the easel, and his (Drioli's) own wife standing in the center of the room, posing for her picture.

"Tonight we shall celebrate," he said. "We shall have a little celebration, us three."

"What is it that we celebrate?" the boy asked, without looking up. "Is it that you have decided to divorce your wife so she can marry me?"

"No," Drioli said. "We celebrate because today I have made a great sum of money with my work."

"And I have made nothing. We can celebrate that also."

"If you like." Drioli was standing by the table unwrapping the parcel. He felt tired and he wanted to get at the wine. Nine clients in one day was all very nice, but it could play hell with a man's eyes. He had never done as many as nine before. Nine boozy soldiers—and the remarkable thing was that no fewer than seven of them had been able to pay in cash. This had made him extremely rich. But the work was terrible on the eyes. Drioli's eyes were half closed from fatigue, the whites streaked with little connecting lines of red; and about an inch behind each eyeball there was a small concentration of pain. But it was evening now and he was wealthy as a pig, and in the parcel there were three bottles—one for his wife, one for his friend, and one for him. He had found the corkscrew and was drawing the corks from the bottles, each making a small plop as it came out.

The boy put down his brush. "Oh, Christ," he said. "How can one work with all this going on?"

The girl came across the room to look at the painting. Drioli came over also, holding a bottle in one hand, a glass in the other.

"No," the boy shouted, blazing up suddenly. "Please—no!" He snatched the canvas from the easel and stood it against the wall. But Drioli had seen it.

"I like it."

"It's terrible."

"It's marvelous. Like all the others that you do, it's marvelous. I love them all."

"The trouble is," the boy said, scowling, "that in themselves they are not nourishing. I cannot eat them."

"But still they are marvelous." Drioli handed him a tumblerful of the pale yellow wine. "Drink it," he said. "It will make you happy."

Never, he thought, had he known a more unhappy person, or one with a gloomier face. He had spotted him in a café some seven months before, drinking alone, and because he had looked like a Russian or some sort of an Asiatic, Drioli had sat down at his table and talked.

"You are a Russian?"

"Yes."

"Where from?"

"Minsk."

Drioli had jumped up and embraced him, crying that he too had been born in that city.

"It wasn't actually Minsk," the boy had said. "But quite near."

"Where?"

"Smilovichi, about twelve miles away."

"Smilovichi!" Drioli had shouted, embracing him again. "I walked there several times when I was a boy." Then he had sat down again, staring affectionately at the other's face. "You know," he had said, "you don't look like a western Russian. You're like a Tartar, or a Kalmuck. You look exactly like a Kalmuck."

Now, standing in the studio, Drioli looked again at the boy as he took the glass of wine and tipped it down his throat in one swallow. Yes, he did have a face like a Kalmuck—very broad and high-cheeked, with a wide coarse nose. This broadness of the cheeks was accentuated by the ears which stood out sharply from the head. And then he had the narrow eyes, the black hair, the thick sullen mouth of a Kalmuck, but the hands—the hands were always a surprise, so small and white like a lady's, with tiny thin fingers.

"Give me some more," the boy said. "If we are to celebrate then let us do it properly."

Drioli distributed the wine and sat himself on a chair. The boy sat on the old couch with Drioli's wife. The three bottles were placed on the floor between them.

"Tonight we shall drink as much as we possibly can," Drioli said. "I am exceptionally rich. I think perhaps I should go out now and buy some more bottles. How many shall I get?"

"Six more," the boy said. "Two for each."

"Good. I shall go now and fetch them."

"And I will help you."

In the nearest café Drioli bought six bottles of white wine, and then carried them back to the studio. They placed them on the floor in two rows, and Drioli fetched the corkscrew and pulled the corks, all six of them; then they sat down again and continued to drink.

"It is only the very wealthy," Drioli said, "who can afford to cele-brate in this manner."

"That is true," the boy said. "Isn't that true, Josie?"

"Of course."

"How do you feel, Josie?"

"Fine."

"Will you leave Drioli and marry me?"

"No."

"Beautiful wine," Drioli said. "It is a privilege to drink it."

Slowly, methodically, they set about getting themselves drunk. The process was routine, but all the same there was a certain ceremony to be observed, and a gravity to be maintained, and a great number of things to be said, then said again—and the wine must be praised, and the slowness was important too, so that there would be time to savour the three delicious stages of transition, especially (for Drioli) the one when he began to float and his feet did not really belong to him. That was the best period of them all—when he could look down at his feet and they were so far away that he would wonder what crazy person they might belong to and why they were lying around on the floor like that, in the distance.

After a while, he got up to switch on the light. He was surprised to see that the feet came with him when he did this, especially because he couldn't feel them touching the ground. It gave him a pleasant sensa-tion of walking on air. Then he began wandering around the room, peeking slyly at the canvases stacked against the walls.

"Listen," he said at length. "I have an idea." He came across and stood before the couch, swaying gently. "Listen, my little Kalmuck."

"What?"

"I have a tremendous idea. Are you listening?"

"I'm listening to Josie."

"Listen to me, *please*. You are my friend—my ugly little Kalmuck from Minsk—and to me you are such an artist that I would like to have a picture, a lovely picture—"

"Have them all. Take all you can find, but do not interrupt me when I am talking with your wife."

"No, no. Now listen. I mean a picture that I can have with me always . . . for ever . . . wherever I go . . . whatever happens . . . but always with me . . . a picture by you." He reached forward and shook the boy's knee. "Now listen to me, *please*."

"Listen to him," the girl said.

"It is this. I want you to paint a picture on my skin, on my back. Then I want you to tattoo over what you have painted so that it will be there always."

"You have crazy ideas."

"I will teach you how to use the tattoo. It is easy. A child could do it."

"I am not a child."

"Please . . ."

"You are quite mad. What is it you want?" The painter looked up into the slow, dark, wine-bright eyes of the other man. "What in heaven's name is it you want?"

"You could do it easily! You could! You could!"

"You mean with the tattoo?"

"Yes, with the tattoo! I will teach you in two minutes!"

"Impossible!"

"Are you saying I do not know what I am talking about?"

No, the boy could not possibly be saying that because if anyone knew about the tattoo it was he—Drioli. Had he not, only last month, covered a man's whole belly with the most wonderful and delicate design composed entirely of flowers? What about the client who had had so much hair upon his chest that he had done him a picture of a grizzly bear so designed that the hair on the chest became the furry coat of the bear? Could he not draw the likeness of a lady and position it with such subtlety upon a man's arm that when the muscle of the arm was flexed the lady came to life and performed some astonishing contortions?

"All I am saying," the boy told him, "is that you are drunk and this is a drunken idea."

"We could have Josie for a model. A study of Josie upon my back. Am I not entitled to a picture of my wife upon my back?"

"Of Josie?"

"Yes." Drioli knew he only had to mention his wife and the boy's thick brown lips would loosen and begin to quiver.

"No," the girl said.

"Darling Josie, *please*. Take this bottle and finish it, then you will feel more generous. It is an enormous idea. Never in my life have I had such an idea before."

"What idea?"

"That he should make a picture of you upon my back. Am I not entitled to that?"

"A picture of me?"

"A nude study," the boy said. "It is an agreeable idea."

"Not nude," the girl said.

"It is an enormous idea," Drioli said.

"It's a damn crazy idea," the girl said.

"It is in any event an idea," the boy said. "It is an idea that calls for a celebration."

They emptied another bottle among them. Then the boy said, "It is no good. I could not possibly manage the tattoo. Instead, I will paint this picture on your back and you will have it with you so long as you do not take a bath and wash it off. If you never take a bath again in your life then you will have it always, as long as you live."

"No," Drioli said.

"Yes—and on the day that you decide to take a bath I will know that you do not any longer value my picture. It will be a test of your admiration for my art."

"I do not like the idea," the girl said. "His admiration for your art is so great that he would be unclean for many years. Let us have the tattoo. But not nude."

"Then just the head," Drioli said.

"I could not manage it."

"It is immensely simple. I will undertake to teach you in two minutes. You will see. I shall go now and fetch the instruments. The needles and the inks. I have inks of many different colors—as many different colors as you have paints, and far more beautiful . . ."

"It is impossible."

"I have many inks. Have I not many different colors of inks, Josie?"

"Yes."

"You will see," Drioli said. "I will go now and fetch them." He got up from his chair and walked unsteadily, but with determination, out of the room.

In half an hour Drioli was back. "I have brought everything," he cried, waving a brown suitcase. "All the necessities of the tattooist are here in this bag."

He placed the bag on the table, opened it, and laid out the electric needles and the small bottles of colored inks. He plugged in the electric needle, then he took the instrument in his hand and pressed a switch. It made a buzzing sound and the quarter inch of needle that projected from the end of it began to vibrate swiftly up and down. He threw off his jacket and rolled up his sleeve. "Now look. Watch me and I will show you how easy it is. I will make a design on my arm, here."

His forearm was already covered with blue markings, but he selected a small clear patch of skin upon which to demonstrate.

"First, I choose my ink—let us use ordinary blue—and I dip the point of the needle in the ink . . . so . . . and I hold the needle up straight and I run it lightly over the surface of the skin . . . like this . . . and with the little motor and the electricity, the needle jumps up and down and punctures the skin and the ink goes in and there you are. See how easy it is . . . see how I draw a picture of a greyhound here upon my arm . . ."

The boy was intrigued. "Now let *me* practice a little—on your arm."

With the buzzing needle he began to draw blue lines upon Drioli's arm. "It is simple," he said. "It is like drawing with pen and ink. There is no difference except that it is slower."

"There is nothing to it. Are you ready? Shall we begin?"

"At once."

"The model!" cried Drioli. "Come on, Josie!" He was in a bustle of enthusiasm now, tottering around the room arranging everything, like a child preparing for some exciting game. "Where will you have her? Where shall she stand?"

"Let her be standing there, by my dressing-table. Let her be brushing her hair. I will paint her with her hair down over her shoulders and her brushing it."

"Tremendous. You are a genius."

Reluctantly, the girl walked over and stood by the dressing table, carrying her glass of wine with her.

Drioli pulled off his shirt and stepped out of his trousers. He retained only his underpants and his socks and shoes, and he stood there swaying gently from side to side, his small body firm, white-skinned, almost hairless. "Now," he said, "I am the canvas. Where will you place your canvas?"

"As always, upon the easel."

"Don't be crazy. I am the canvas."

"Then place yourself upon the easel. That is where you belong."

"How can I?"

"Are you the canvas or are you not the canvas?"

"I am the canvas. Already I begin to feel like a canvas."

"Then place yourself upon the easel. There should be no difficulty."

"Truly, it is not possible."

"Then sit on the chair. Sit back to front, then you can lean your drunken head against the back of it. Hurry now, for I am about to commence."

"I am ready. I am waiting."

"First," the boy said, "I shall make an ordinary painting. Then, if it pleases me, I shall tattoo over it." With a wide brush he began to paint upon the naked skin of the man's back.

"Ayee! Ayee!" Drioli screamed. "A monstrous centipede is marching down my spine!"

"Be still now! Be still!" The boy worked rapidly, applying the paint only in a thin blue wash so that it would not afterwards interfere with the process of tattooing. His concentration, as soon as he began to paint, was so great that it appeared somehow to supersede his drunkenness. He applied the brush strokes with quick jabs of the arm, holding the wrist stiff, and in less than half an hour it was finished.

"All right. That's all," he said to the girl, who immediately returned to the couch, lay down, and fell asleep.

Drioli remained awake. He watched the boy take up the needle and dip it in the ink; then he felt the sharp tickling sting as it touched the skin of his back. The pain, which was unpleasant but never extreme, kept him from going to sleep. By following the track of the needle and by watching the different colors of ink that the boy was using, Drioli amused himself trying to visualize what was going on behind him. The boy worked with an astonishing intensity. He appeared to have become completely absorbed in the little machine and in the unusual effects it was able to produce.

Far into the small hours of the morning the machine buzzed and the boy worked. Drioli could remember that when the artist finally stepped back and said, "It is finished," there was daylight outside and the sound of people walking in the street.

"I want to see it," Drioli said. The boy held up a mirror, at an angle, and Drioli craned his neck to look.

"Good God!" he cried. It was a startling sight. The whole of his back, from the top of the shoulders to the base of the spine, was a blaze of color—gold and green and blue and black and scarlet. The tattoo was applied so heavily it looked almost like an impasto. The boy had followed as closely as possible the original brush strokes, filling them in solid, and it was marvelous the way he had made use of the spine and the protrusion of the shoulder blades so that they became part of the composition. What is more, he had somehow managed to achieve— even with this slow process—a certain spontaneity. The portrait was quite alive; it contained much of that twisted, tortured quality so characteristic of Soutine's other work. It was not a good likeness. It was a mood rather than a likeness, the model's face vague and tipsy, the background swirling around her head in a mass of dark green curling strokes.

"It's tremendous!"

"I rather like it myself." The boy stood back, examining it critically. "You know," he added, "I think it's good enough for me to sign." And taking up the buzzer again, he inscribed his name in red ink on the right-hand side, over the place where Drioli's kidney was.

The old man who was called Drioli was standing in a sort of trance, staring at the painting in the window of the picture-dealer's shop. It had been so long ago, all that—almost as though it had happened in another life.

And the boy? What had become of him? He could remember now that after returning from the war—the first war—he had missed him and had questioned Josie.

"Where is my little Kalmuck?"

"He is gone," she had answered. "I do not know where, but I heard it said that a dealer had taken him up and sent him away to Céret to make more paintings."

"Perhaps he will return."

"Perhaps he will. Who knows?"

That was the last time they had mentioned him. Shortly afterwards they had moved to Le Havre where there were more sailors and business was better. The old man smiled as he remembered Le Havre. Those were the pleasant years, the years between the wars, with the small shop near the docks and the comfortable rooms and always enough work, with every day three, four, five sailors coming and wanting pictures on their arms. Those were truly the pleasant years.

Then had come the second war, and Josie being killed, and the Germans arriving, and that was the finish of his business. No one had wanted pictures on their arms any more after that. And by that time he was too old for any other kind of work. In desperation he had made his way back to Paris, hoping vaguely that things would be easier in the big city. But they were not.

And now, after the war was over, he possessed neither the means nor the energy to start up his small business again. It wasn't very easy for an old man to know what to do, especially when one did not like to beg. Yet how else could he keep alive?

Well, he thought, still staring at the picture. So that is my little Kalmuck. And how quickly the sight of one small object such as this can stir the memory. Up to a few moments ago he had even forgotten that he had a tattoo on his back. It had been ages since he had thought about it. He put his face closer to the window and looked into the gallery. On the walls he could see many other pictures and all seemed to be the work of the same artist. There were a great number of people strolling around. Obviously it was a special exhibition.

On a sudden impulse, Drioli turned, pushed open the door of the gallery and went in.

It was a long room with thick wine-colored carpet, and by God how beautiful and warm it was! There were all these people strolling about looking at the pictures, well-washed dignified people, each of whom held a catalog in the hand. Drioli stood just inside the door, nervously glancing around, wondering whether he dared go forward and mingle with this crowd. But before he had had time to gather his courage, he heard a voice beside him saying, "What is it you want?"

The speaker wore a black morning coat. He was plump and short and had a very white face. It was a flabby face with so much flesh upon it that the cheeks hung down on either side of the mouth in two fleshy collops, spanielwise. He came up close to Drioli and said again, "What is it you want?"

Drioli stood still.

"If you please," the man was saying, "take yourself out of my gallery."

"Am I not permitted to look at the pictures?"

"I have asked you to leave."

Drioli stood his ground. He felt suddenly overwhelmingly outraged.

"Let us not have trouble," the man was saying. "Come on now, this way." He put a fat white paw on Drioli's arm and began to push him firmly to the door.

That did it. "Take your goddam hands off me!" Drioli shouted. His voice rang clear down the long gallery and all the heads jerked around as one—all the startled faces stared down the length of the room at the person who had made this noise. A flunkey came running over to help, and the two men tried to hustle Drioli through the door. The people stood still, watching the struggle. Their faces expressed only a mild interest, and seemed to be saying, "It's all right. There's no danger to us. It's being taken care of."

"I, too!" Drioli was shouting, "I, too, have a picture by this painter! He was my friend and I have a picture which he gave me!"

"He's mad."

"A lunatic. A raving lunatic."

"Someone should call the police."

With a rapid twist of the body Drioli suddenly jumped clear of the two men, and before anyone could stop him he was running down the gallery shouting, "I'll show you! I'll show you! I'll show you!" He flung off his overcoat, then his jacket and shirt, and he turned so that his naked back was towards the people.

"There!" he cried, breathing quickly. "You see? There it is!"

There was a sudden absolute silence in the room, each person arrested in what he was doing, standing motionless in a kind of shocked, uneasy bewilderment. They were staring at the tattooed picture. It was still there, the colors as bright as ever, but the old man's back was thinner now, the shoulder blades protruded more sharply, and the effect, though not great, was to give the picture a curiously wrinkled, squashed appearance.

Somebody said, "My God, but it is!"

Then came the excitement and the noise of voices as the people surged forward to crowd around the old man.

"It is unmistakable!"

"His early manner, yes?"

"It is fantastic, fantastic!"

"And look, it is signed!"

"Bend your shoulders forward, my friend, so that the picture stretches out flat."

"Old one, when was this done?"

"In 1913," Drioli said, without turning around. "In the autumn of 1913."

"Who taught Soutine to tattoo?"

"I taught him."

"And the woman?"

"She was my wife."

The gallery owner was pushing through the crowd towards Drioli. He was calm now, deadly serious, making a smile with his mouth. "Monsieur," he said, "I will buy it." Drioli could see the loose fat upon the face vibrating as he moved his jaw. "I said I will buy it, Monsieur."

"How can you buy it?" Drioli asked softly.

"I will give two hundred thousand francs for it." The dealer's eyes were small and dark, the wings of his broad nose-base were beginning to quiver.

"Don't do it!" someone murmured in the crowd. "It is worth twenty times as much."

Drioli opened his mouth to speak. No words came, so he shut it; then he opened it again and said slowly, "But how can I sell it?" He lifted his hands, let them drop loosely to his sides. "Monsieur, how can I possibly sell it?" All the sadness in the world was in his voice.

"Yes!" they were saying in the crowd. "How can he sell it? It is part of himself!"

"Listen," the dealer said, coming up close. "I will help you, I will make you rich. Together we shall make some private arrangement over this picture, no?"

Drioli watched him with slow, apprehensive eyes. "But how can you buy it, Monsieur? What will you do with it when you have bought it? Where will you keep it? Where will you keep it tonight? And where tomorrow?"

"Ah, where will I keep it? Yes, where will I keep it? Now, where will I keep it? Well, now . . ." The dealer stroked the bridge of his nose with a fat white finger. "It would seem," he said, "that if I take the picture, I take you also. That is a disadvantage." He paused and stroked his nose again. "The picture itself is of no value until you are dead. How old are you, my friend?"

"Sixty-one."

"But you are perhaps not very robust, no?" The dealer lowered the hand from his nose and looked Drioli up and down, slowly, like a farmer appraising an old horse.

"I do not like this," Drioli said, edging away. "Quite honestly, Monsieur, I do not like it." He edged straight into the arms of a tall man who put out his hands and caught him gently by the shoulders. Drioli glanced around and apologized. The man smiled down at him, patting one of the old fellow's naked shoulders reassuringly with a hand encased in a canary-colored glove.

"Listen, my friend," the stranger said, still smiling. "Do you like to swim and to bask yourself in the sun?"

Drioli looked up at him, rather startled.

"Do you like fine food and red wine from the great chateaux of Bordeaux?" The man was still smiling, showing strong white teeth with a flash of gold among them. He spoke in a soft coaxing manner, one gloved hand still resting on Drioli's shoulder. "Do you like such things?"

"Well—yes," Drioli answered, still greatly perplexed. "Of course."

"And the company of beautiful women?"

"Why not?"

SKIN

"And a cupboard full of suits and shirts made to your own personal measurements? It would seem that you are a little lacking for clothes."

Drioli watched this suave man, waiting for the rest of the proposition.

"Have you ever had a shoe constructed especially for your own foot?"

"No."

"You would like that?"

"Well . . ."

"And a man who will shave you in the mornings and trim your hair?"

Drioli simply stood and gaped.

"And a plump attractive girl to manicure the nails of your fingers?"

Someone in the crowd giggled.

"And a bell beside your bed to summon your maid to bring your breakfast in the morning? Would you like these things, my friend? Do they appeal to you?"

Drioli stood still and looked at him.

"You see, I am the owner of the Hotel Bristol in Cannes. I now invite you to come down there and live as my guest for the rest of your life in luxury and comfort." The man paused, allowing his listener time to savor this cheerful prospect.

"Your only duty—shall I call it your pleasure—will be to spend your time on my beach in bathing trunks, walking among my guests, sunning yourself, swimming, drinking cocktails. You would like that?"

There was no answer.

"Don't you see—all the guests will thus be able to observe this fascinating picture by Soutine. You will become famous, and men will say,

'Look, there is the fellow with ten million francs upon his back.' You like this idea, Monsieur? It pleases you?"

Drioli looked up at the tall man in the canary gloves, still wondering whether this was some sort of a joke. "It is a comical idea," he said slowly. "But do you really mean it?"

"Of course I mean it."

"Wait," the dealer interrupted. "See here, old one. Here is the answer to our problem. I will buy the picture, and I will arrange with a surgeon to remove the skin from your back, and then you will be able to go off on your own and enjoy the great sum of money I shall give you for it."

"With no skin on my back?"

"No, no, please! You misunderstand. This surgeon will put a new piece of skin in the place of the old one. It is simple."

"Could he do that?"

"There is nothing to it."

"Impossible!" said the man with the canary gloves. "He's too old for such a major skin-grafting operation. It would kill him. It would kill you, my friend."

"It would kill me?"

"Naturally. You would never survive. Only the picture would come through."

"In the name of God!" Drioli cried. He looked around aghast at the faces of the people watching him, and in the silence that followed, another man's voice, speaking quietly from the back of the group, could be heard saying, "Perhaps, if one were to offer this old man enough money, he might consent to kill himself on the spot. Who knows?" A few people sniggered. The dealer moved his feet uneasily on the carpet.

Then the hand in the canary glove was tapping Drioli again upon the shoulder. "Come on," the man was saying, smiling his broad white smile. "You and I will go and have a good dinner and we can talk about it some more while we eat. How's that? Are you hungry?"

Drioli watched him, frowning. He didn't like the man's long flexible neck, or the way he craned it forward at you when he spoke, like a snake.

"Roast duck and Chambertin," the man was saying. He put a rich succulent accent on the words, splashing them out with his tongue. "And perhaps a soufflé aux marrons, light and frothy."

Drioli's eyes turned up towards the ceiling, his lips became loose and wet. One could see the poor old fellow beginning literally to drool at the mouth.

"How do you like your duck?" the man went on. "Do you like it very brown and crisp outside, or shall it be . . ."

"I am coming," Drioli said quickly. Already he had picked up his shirt and was pulling it frantically over his head. "Wait for me, Monsieur. I am coming." And within a minute he had disappeared out of the gallery with his new patron.

It wasn't more than a few weeks later that a picture by Soutine, of a woman's head, painted in an unusual manner, nicely framed and heavily varnished, turned up for sale in Buenos Aires. That—and the fact that there is no hotel in Cannes called Bristol—causes one to wonder a little, and to pray for the old man's health, and to hope fervently that wherever he may be at this moment, there is a plump attractive girl to manicure the nails of his fingers, and a maid to bring him his breakfast in bed in the mornings.

LAMB TO THE SLAUGHTER

The room was warm and clean, the curtains drawn, the two table lamps alight—hers and the one by the empty chair opposite. On the sideboard behind her, two tall glasses, soda water, whiskey. Fresh ice cubes in the Thermos bucket.

Mary Maloney was waiting for her husband to come home from work.

Now and again she would glance up at the clock, but without anxiety, merely to please herself with the thought that each minute gone by made it nearer the time when he would come. There was a slow smiling air about her, and about everything she did. The drop of the head as she bent over her sewing was curiously tranquil. Her skin—for this was her sixth month with child—had acquired a wonderful translucent quality, the mouth was soft, and the eyes, with their new placid look, seemed larger, darker than before.

When the clock said ten minutes to five, she began to listen, and a few moments later, punctually as always, she heard the tires on the gravel outside, and the car door slamming, the footsteps passing the window, the key turning in the lock. She laid aside her sewing, stood up, and went forward to kiss him as he came in.

"Hullo, darling," she said.

"Hullo," he answered.

She took his coat and hung it in the closet. Then she walked over and made the drinks, a strongish one for him, a weak one for herself; and soon she was back again in her chair with the sewing, and he in the other, opposite, holding the tall glass with both his hands, rocking it so the ice cubes tinkled against the side.

For her, this was always a blissful time of day. She knew he didn't want to speak much until the first drink was finished, and she, on her side, was content to sit quietly, enjoying his company after the long hours alone in the house. She loved to luxuriate in the presence of this man, and to feel—almost as a sunbather feels the sun—that warm male glow that came out of him to her when they were alone together. She loved him for the way he sat loosely in a chair, for the way he came in a door, or moved slowly across the room with long strides. She loved the intent, far look in his eyes when they rested on her, the funny shape of the mouth, and especially the way he remained silent about his tiredness, sitting still with himself until the whiskey had taken some of it away.

"Tired, darling?"

"Yes," he said. "I'm tired." And as he spoke, he did an unusual thing. He lifted his glass and drained it in one swallow although there was still half of it, at least half of it, left. She wasn't really watching him but she knew what he had done because she heard the ice cubes falling back against the bottom of the empty glass when he lowered his arm. He paused a moment, leaning forward in the chair, then he got up and went slowly over to fetch himself another.

"I'll get it!" she cried, jumping up.

"Sit down," he said.

When he came back, she noticed that the new drink was dark amber with the quantity of whiskey in it.

"Darling, shall I get your slippers?"

"No."

She watched him as he began to sip the dark yellow drink, and she could see little oily swirls in the liquid because it was so strong.

"I think it's a shame," she said, "that when a policeman gets to be as senior as you, they keep him walking about on his feet all day long."

He didn't answer, so she bent her head again and went on with her sewing; but each time he lifted the drink to his lips, she heard the ice cubes clinking against the side of the glass.

"Darling," she said. "Would you like me to get you some cheese? I haven't made any supper because it's Thursday."

"No," he said.

"If you're too tired to eat out," she went on, "it's still not too late. There's plenty of meat and stuff in the freezer, and you can have it right here and not even move out of the chair."

Her eyes waited on him for an answer, a smile, a little nod, but he made no sign.

"Anyway," she went on, "I'll get you some cheese and crackers first."

"I don't want it," he said.

She moved uneasily in her chair, the large eyes still watching his face. "But you *must* have supper. I can easily do it here. I'd like to do it. We can have lamb chops. Or pork. Anything you want. Everything's in the freezer."

"Forget it," he said.

"But, darling, you *must* eat! I'll fix it anyway, and then you can have it or not, as you like."

She stood up and placed her sewing on the table by the lamp.

"Sit down," he said. "Just for a minute, sit down."

It wasn't till then that she began to get frightened.

"Go on," he said. "Sit down."

She lowered herself back slowly into the chair, watching him all the time with those large, bewildered eyes. He had finished the second drink and was staring down into the glass frowning.

"Listen," he said, "I've got something to tell you."

"What is it, darling? What's the matter?"

He had become absolutely motionless, and he kept his head down so that the light from the lamp beside him fell across the upper part of his face, leaving the chin and mouth in shadow. She noticed there was a little muscle moving near the corner of his left eye.

"This is going to be a bit of a shock to you, I'm afraid," he said. "But I've thought about it a good deal and I've decided the only thing to do is tell you right away. I hope you won't blame me too much."

And he told her. It didn't take long, four or five minutes at most, and she sat very still through it all, watching him with a kind of dazed horror as he went further and further away from her with each word.

"So there it is," he added. "And I know it's kind of a bad time to be telling you, but there simply wasn't any other way. Of course I'll give you money and see you're looked after. But there needn't really be any fuss. I hope not anyway. It wouldn't be very good for my job."

Her first instinct was not to believe any of it, to reject it all. It occurred to her that perhaps he hadn't even spoken, that she herself had imagined the whole thing. Maybe, if she went about her business and acted as though she hadn't been listening, then later, when she sort of woke up again, she might find none of it had ever happened.

"I'll get the supper," she managed to whisper, and this time he didn't stop her.

When she walked across the room she couldn't feel her feet touching the floor. She couldn't feel anything at all—except a slight nausea and a desire to vomit. Everything was automatic now—down the stairs to the cellar, the light switch, the deep freeze, the hand inside the cabinet taking hold of the first object it met. She lifted it out, and looked at it. It was wrapped in paper, so she took off the paper and looked at it again.

A leg of lamb.

All right then, they would have lamb for supper. She carried it upstairs, holding the thin bone end of it with both her hands, and as she went through the living room, she saw him standing over by the window with his back to her, and she stopped.

"For God's sake," he said, hearing her, but not turning round. "Don't make supper for me. I'm going out."

At that point, Mary Maloney simply walked up behind him and without any pause she swung the big frozen leg of lamb high in the air and brought it down as hard as she could on the back of his head.

She might just as well have hit him with a steel club.

She stepped back a pace, waiting, and the funny thing was that he remained standing there for at least four or five seconds, gently swaying. Then he crashed to the carpet.

The violence of the crash, the noise, the small table overturning, helped bring her out of the shock. She came out slowly, feeling cold and surprised, and she stood for a while blinking at the body, still hold-ing the ridiculous piece of meat tight with both hands.

All right, she told herself. So I've killed him.

It was extraordinary, now, how clear her mind became all of a sud-den. She began thinking very fast. As the wife of a detective, she knew quite well what the penalty would be. That was fine. It made no differ-ence to her. In fact, it would be a relief. On the other hand, what about the child? What were the laws about murderers with unborn children? Did they kill them both—mother and child? Or did they wait until the tenth month? What did they do?

Mary Maloney didn't know. And she certainly wasn't prepared to take a chance.

She carried the meat into the kitchen, placed it in a pan, turned the oven on high, and shoved it inside. Then she washed her hands and ran upstairs to the bedroom. She sat down before the mirror, tidied her face, touched up her lips and face. She tried a smile. It came out rather peculiar. She tried again.

"Hullo, Sam," she said brightly, aloud.

The voice sounded peculiar too.

"I want some potatoes please, Sam. Yes, and I think a can of peas."

That was better. Both the smile and the voice were coming out bet-ter now. She rehearsed it several times more. Then she ran downstairs, took her coat, went out the back door, down the garden, into the street.

It wasn't six o'clock yet and the lights were still on in the grocery shop.

"Hullo, Sam," she said brightly, smiling at the man behind the counter.

"Why, good evening, Mrs. Maloney. How're *you?*"

"I want some potatoes please, Sam. Yes, and I think a can of peas."

The man turned and reached up behind him on the shelf for the peas.

"Patrick's decided he's tired and doesn't want to eat out tonight," she told him. "We usually go out Thursdays, you know, and now he's caught me without any vegetables in the house."

"Then how about meat, Mrs. Maloney?"

"No, I've got meat, thanks. I got a nice leg of lamb, from the freezer."

"Oh."

"I don't much like cooking it frozen, Sam, but I'm taking a chance on it this time. You think it'll be all right?"

"Personally," the grocer said, "I don't believe it makes any difference. You want these Idaho potatoes?"

"Oh yes, that'll be fine. Two of those."

"Anything else?" The grocer cocked his head on one side, looking at her pleasantly. "How about afterwards? What you going to give him for afterwards?"

"Well—what would you suggest, Sam?"

The man glanced around his shop. "How about a nice big slice of cheesecake? I know he likes that."

"Perfect," she said. "He loves it."

And when it was all wrapped and she had paid she put on her brightest smile and said, "Thank you, Sam. Good night."

"Good night, Mrs. Maloney. And thank *you*."

And now, she told herself as she hurried back, all she was doing now, she was returning home to her husband and he was waiting for his supper; and she must cook it good, and make it as tasty as possible because the poor man was tired; and if, when she entered the house, she happened to find anything unusual, or tragic, or terrible, then naturally it would be a shock and she'd become frantic with grief and horror. Mind you, she wasn't *expecting* to find anything. She was just going home with the vegetables. Mrs. Patrick Maloney going home with the vegetables on Thursday evening to cook supper for her husband.

That's the way, she told herself. Do everything right and natural. Keep things absolutely natural and there'll be no need for any acting at all.

Therefore, when she entered the kitchen by the back door, she was humming a little tune to herself and smiling.

"Patrick!" she called. "How are you, darling?"

She put the parcel down on the table and went through into the living room; and when she saw him lying there on the floor with his legs doubled up and one arm twisted back underneath his body, it really was rather a shock. All the old love and longing for him welled up inside her, and she ran over to him, knelt down beside him, and began to cry her heart out. It was easy. No acting was necessary.

A few minutes later she got up and went to the phone. She knew the number of the police station, and when the man at the other end answered, she cried to him, "Quick! Come quick! Patrick's dead!"

"Who's speaking?"

"Mrs. Maloney. Mrs. Patrick Maloney."

"You mean Patrick Maloney's dead?"

"I think so," she sobbed. "He's lying on the floor and I think he's dead."

"Be right over," the man said.

The car came over quickly, and when she opened the front door, two policemen walked in. She knew them both—she knew nearly all the men at that precinct—and she fell right into Jack Noonan's arms, weeping hysterically. He put her gently into a chair, then went over to join the other one, who was called O'Malley, kneeling by the body.

"Is he dead?" she cried.

"I'm afraid he is. What happened?"

Briefly, she told her story about going out to the grocer and coming back to find him on the floor. While she was talking, crying and talking, Noonan discovered a small patch of congealed blood on the dead man's head. He showed it to O'Malley who got up at once and hurried to the phone.

Soon, other men began to come into the house. First a doctor, then two detectives, one of whom she knew by name. Later, a police photographer arrived and took pictures, and a man who knew about fingerprints. There was a great deal of whispering and muttering beside the corpse, and the detectives kept asking her a lot of questions. But they always treated her kindly. She told her story again, this time right from the beginning, when Patrick had come in, and she was sewing, and he was tired, so tired he hadn't wanted to go out for supper. She told how she'd put the meat in the oven—"it's there now, cooking"— and how she'd slipped out to the grocer for vegetables, and come back to find him lying on the floor.

"Which grocer?" one of the detectives asked.

She told him, and he turned and whispered something to the other detective who immediately went outside into the street.

In fifteen minutes he was back with a page of notes, and there was more whispering, and through her sobbing she heard a few of the whispered phrases—". . . acted quite normal . . . very cheerful . . . wanted to give him a good supper . . . peas . . . cheesecake . . . impossible that she . . ."

After a while, the photographer and the doctor departed and two other men came in and took the corpse away on a stretcher. Then the fingerprint man went away. The two detectives remained, and so did the two policemen. They were exceptionally nice to her, and Jack Noonan asked if she wouldn't rather go somewhere else, to her sister's house perhaps, or to his own wife who would take care of her and put her up for the night.

No, she said. She didn't feel she could move even a yard at the moment. Would they mind awfully if she stayed just where she was until she felt better? She didn't feel too good at the moment, she really didn't.

Then hadn't she better lie down on the bed? Jack Noonan asked.

No, she said, she'd like to stay right where she was, in this chair. A little later perhaps, when she felt better, she would move.

So they left her there while they went about their business, searching the house. Occasionally one of the detectives asked her another question. Sometimes Jack Noonan spoke to her gently as he passed by. Her husband, he told her, had been killed by a blow on the back of the head administered with a heavy blunt instrument, almost certainly a large piece of metal. They were looking for the weapon. The murderer may have taken it with him, but on the other hand he may've thrown it away or hidden it somewhere on the premises.

"It's the old story," he said. "Get the weapon, and you've got the man."

Later, one of the detectives came up and sat beside her. Did she know, he asked, of anything in the house that could've been used as the weapon? Would she mind having a look around to see if anything was missing—a very big spanner for example, or a heavy metal vase.

They didn't have any heavy metal vases, she said.

"Or a big spanner?"

She didn't think they had a big spanner. But there might be some things like that in the garage.

The search went on. She knew that there were other policemen in the garden all around the house. She could hear their footsteps on the gravel outside, and sometimes she saw the flash of a torch through a chink in the curtains. It began to get late, nearly nine she noticed by the clock on the mantel. The four men searching the rooms seemed to be growing weary, a trifle exasperated.

"Jack," she said, the next time Sergeant Noonan went by. "Would you mind giving me a drink?"

"Sure I'll give you a drink. You mean this whiskey?"

"Yes, please. But just a small one. It might make me feel better."

He handed her the glass.

"Why don't you have one yourself," she said. "You must be awfully tired. Please do. You've been very good to me."

"Well," he answered. "It's not strictly allowed, but I might take just a drop to keep me going."

One by one the others came in and were persuaded to take a little nip of whiskey. They stood around rather awkwardly with the drinks in their hands, uncomfortable in her presence, trying to say consoling things to her. Sergeant Noonan wandered into the kitchen, came out quickly and said, "Look, Mrs. Maloney. You know that oven of yours is still on, and the meat still inside."

"Oh *dear* me!" she cried. "So it is!"

"I better turn it off for you, hadn't I?"

"Will you do that, Jack. Thank you so much."

When the sergeant returned the second time, she looked at him with her large, dark, tearful eyes. "Jack Noonan," she said.

"Yes?"

"Would you do me a small favor—you and these others?"

"We can try, Mrs. Maloney."

"Well," she said. "Here you all are, and good friends of dear Patrick's too, and helping to catch the man who killed him. You must be terribly hungry by now because it's long past your supper time, and I know Patrick would never forgive me, God bless his soul, if I allowed you to remain in his house without offering you decent hospitality. Why don't you eat up that lamb that's in the oven? It'll be cooked just right by now."

"Wouldn't dream of it," Sergeant Noonan said.

"Please," she begged. "Please eat it. Personally I couldn't touch a thing, certainly not what's been in the house when he was here. But it's all right for you. It'd be a favor to me if you'd eat it up. Then you can go on with your work again afterwards."

There was a good deal of hesitating among the four policemen, but they were clearly hungry, and in the end they were persuaded to go into the kitchen and help themselves. The woman stayed where she was, listening to them through the open door, and she could hear them speaking among themselves, their voices thick and sloppy because their mouths were full of meat.

"Have some more, Charlie?"

"No. Better not finish it."

ROALD DAHL

"She *wants* us to finish it. She said so. Be doing her a favor."

"Okay then. Give me some more."

"That's the hell of a big club the guy must've used to hit poor Patrick," one of them was saying. "The doc says his skull was smashed all to pieces just like from a sledgehammer."

"That's why it ought to be easy to find."

"Exactly what I say."

"Whoever done it, they're not going to be carrying a thing like that around with them longer than they need."

One of them belched.

"Personally, I think it's right here on the premises."

"Probably right under our very noses. What you think, Jack?"

And in the other room, Mary Maloney began to giggle.

THE SOUND MACHINE

It was a warm summer evening and Klausner walked quickly through the front gate and around the side of the house and into the garden at the back. He went on down the garden until he came to a wooden shed, and he unlocked the door, went inside, and closed the door behind him.

The interior of the shed was an unpainted room. Against one wall, on the left, there was a long wooden workbench, and on it, among a littering of wires and batteries and small sharp tools, there stood a black box about three feet long, the shape of a child's coffin.

Klausner moved across the room to the box. The top of the box was open, and he bent down and began to poke and peer inside it among a mass of different-colored wires and silver tubes. He picked up a piece of paper that lay beside the box, studied it carefully, put it down, peered inside the box and started running his fingers along the wires, tugging gently at them to test the connections, glancing back at the paper, then into the box, then at the paper again, checking each wire. He did this for perhaps an hour.

Then he put a hand around to the front of the box where there were three dials, and he began to twiddle them, watching at the same time the movement of the mechanism inside the box. All the while he kept speaking softly to himself, nodding his head, smiling sometimes, his hands always moving, the fingers moving swiftly, deftly, inside the box, his mouth twisting into curious shapes when a thing was delicate or difficult to do, saying, "Yes . . . Yes . . . And now this one . . . Yes . . . Yes. But is this right? Is it—where's my diagram? . . . Ah, yes . . . Of course . . . Yes, yes . . . That's right . . . And now . . . Good . . . Good . . . Yes . . . Yes, yes, yes." His concentration was intense; his movements were quick; there was an air of urgency about the way he worked, of breathlessness, of strong suppressed excitement.

Suddenly he heard footsteps on the gravel path outside and he straightened and turned swiftly as the door opened and a tall man came in. It was Scott. It was only Scott, the doctor.

"Well, well, well," the doctor said. "So this is where you hide yourself in the evenings."

"Hullo, Scott," Klausner said.

"I happened to be passing," the doctor told him, "so I dropped in to see how you were. There was no one in the house, so I came on down here. How's that throat of yours been behaving?"

"It's all right. It's fine."

"Now I'm here I might as well have a look at it."

"Please don't trouble. I'm quite cured. I'm fine."

The doctor began to feel the tension in the room. He looked at the black box on the bench; then he looked at the man. "You've got your hat on," he said.

"Oh, have I?" Klausner reached up, removed the hat and put it on the bench.

The doctor came up closer and bent down to look into the box. "What's this?" he said. "Making a radio?"

"No, just fooling around."

"It's got rather complicated-looking innards."

"Yes." Klausner seemed tense and distracted.

"What is it?" the doctor asked. "It's rather a frightening-looking thing, isn't it?"

"It's just an idea."

"Yes?"

"It has to do with sound, that's all."

"Good heavens, man! Don't you get enough of that sort of thing all day in your work?"

"I like sound."

"So it seems." The doctor went to the door, turned, and said, "Well, I won't disturb you. Glad your throat's not worrying you any more." But he kept standing there looking at the box, intrigued by the remarkable complexity of its inside, curious to know what this strange patient of his was up to. "What's it really for?" he asked. "You've made me inquisitive."

Klausner looked down at the box, then at the doctor, and he reached up and began gently to scratch the lobe of his right ear. There was a pause. The doctor stood by the door, waiting, smiling.

"All right, I'll tell you, if you're interested." There was another pause, and the doctor could see that Klausner was having trouble about how to begin.

He was shifting from one foot to the other, tugging at the lobe of his ear, looking at his feet, and then at last, slowly, he said, "Well, it's like this . . . the theory is very simple really. The human ear . . . you know that it can't hear everything. There are sounds that are so low-pitched or so high-pitched that it can't hear them."

"Yes," the doctor said. "Yes."

"Well, speaking very roughly any note so high that it has more than fifteen thousand vibrations a second—we can't hear it. Dogs have better ears than us. You know you can buy a whistle whose note is so high-pitched that you can't hear it at all. But a dog can hear it."

"Yes, I've seen one," the doctor said.

"Of course you have. And up the scale, higher than the note of that whistle, there is another note—a vibration if you like, but I prefer to think of it as a note. You can't hear that one either. And above that there is another and another rising right up the scale forever and ever and ever, an endless succession of notes . . . an infinity of notes . . . there is a note—if only our ears could hear it—so high that it vibrates a million times a second . . . and another a million times as high as that . . . and on and on, higher and higher, as far as numbers go, which is . . . infinity . . . eternity . . . beyond the stars."

Klausner was becoming more animated every moment. He was a frail man, nervous and twitchy, with always moving hands. His large head inclined towards his left shoulder as though his neck were not quite strong enough to support it rigidly. His face was smooth and pale, almost white, and the pale gray eyes that blinked and peered from behind a pair of steel spectacles were bewildered, unfocused, remote. He was a frail, nervous, twitchy little man, a moth of a man, dreamy and distracted; suddenly fluttering and animated; and now the doctor, looking at that strange pale face and those pale gray eyes, felt that somehow there was about this little person a quality of distance, of immense immeasurable distance, as though the mind were far away from where the body was.

The doctor waited for him to go on. Klausner sighed and clasped his hands tightly together. "I believe," he said, speaking more slowly now, "that there is a whole world of sound about us all the time that we cannot hear. It is possible that up there in those high-pitched inaudible regions there is a new exciting music being made, with subtle harmonies and fierce grinding discords, a music so powerful that it would drive us mad if only our ears were tuned to hear the sound of it. There may be anything . . . for all we know there may—"

"Yes," the doctor said. "But it's not very probable."

"Why not? Why not?" Klausner pointed to a fly sitting on a small roll of copper wire on the workbench. "You see that fly? What sort of noise is that fly making now? None—that one can hear. But for all we know the creature may be whistling like mad on a very high note, or barking or croaking or singing a song. It's got a mouth, hasn't it? It's got a throat?"

The doctor looked at the fly and he smiled. He was still standing by the door with his hands on the doorknob. "Well," he said. "So you're going to check up on that?"

"Some time ago," Klausner said, "I made a simple instrument that proved to me the existence of many odd inaudible sounds. Often I have sat and watched the needle of my instrument recording the presence of sound vibrations in the air when I myself could hear nothing. And *those* are the sounds I want to listen to. I want to know where they come from and who or what is making them."

"And that machine on the table there," the doctor said, "is that going to allow you to hear these noises?"

"It may. Who knows? So far, I've had no luck. But I've made some changes in it and tonight I'm ready for another trial. This machine," he said, touching it with his hands, "is designed to pick up sound vibrations that are too high-pitched for reception by the human ear, and to convert them to a scale of audible tones. I tune it in, almost like a radio."

"How d'you mean?"

"It isn't complicated. Say I wish to listen to the squeak of a bat. That's a fairly high-pitched sound—about thirty thousand vibrations a second. The average human ear can't quite hear it. Now, if there were a bat flying around this room and I tuned in to thirty thousand on my machine, I would hear the squeaking of that bat very clearly. I would even hear the correct note—F sharp, or B flat, or whatever it might be—but merely at a much *lower pitch*. Don't you understand?"

The doctor looked at the long, black coffin-box. "And you're going to try it tonight?"

"Yes."

"Well, I wish you luck." He glanced at his watch. "My goodness!" he said. "I must fly. Good-bye, and thank you for telling me. I must call again sometime and find out what happened." The doctor went out and closed the door behind him.

For a while longer, Klausner fussed about with the wires in the black box; then he straightened up and in a soft excited whisper said, "Now we'll try again . . . We'll take it out into the garden this time . . . and then perhaps . . . perhaps . . . the reception will be better. Lift it up now . . . carefully . . . Oh, my God, it's heavy!" He carried the box to the door, found that he couldn't open the door without putting it down, carried it back, put it on the bench, opened the door, and then carried it with some difficulty into the garden. He placed the box carefully on a small wooden table that stood on the lawn. He returned to the shed and fetched a pair of earphones. He plugged the wire connections from the earphones into the machine and put the earphones over his ears. The movements of his hands were quick and precise. He was excited, and breathed loudly and quickly through his mouth. He kept on talking to himself with little words of comfort and encouragement, as though he were afraid—afraid that the machine might not work and afraid also of what might happen if it did.

He stood there in the garden beside the wooden table, so pale, small, and thin that he looked like an ancient, consumptive, bespectacled child. The sun had gone down. There was no wind, no sound at all. From where he stood, he could see over a low fence into the next garden, and there was a woman walking down the garden with a flower basket on her arm. He watched her for a while without thinking about her at all. Then he turned to the box on the table and pressed a switch on its front. He put his left hand on the volume control and his right hand on the knob that moved a needle across a large central dial, like the wavelength dial of a radio. The dial was marked with many numbers, in a series of bands, starting at 15,000 and going on up to 1,000,000.

And now he was bending forward over the machine. His head was cocked to one side in a tense, listening attitude. His right hand was beginning to turn the knob. The needle was traveling slowly across the dial, so slowly he could hardly see it move, and in the earphones he could hear a faint, spasmodic crackling.

Behind this crackling sound he could hear a distant humming tone which was the noise of the machine itself, but that was all. As he listened, he became conscious of a curious sensation, a feeling that his ears were stretching out away from his head, that each ear was connected to his head by a thin stiff wire, like a tentacle, and that the wires were lengthening, that the ears were going up and up towards a secret and forbidden territory, a dangerous ultrasonic region where ears had never been before and had no right to be.

The little needle crept slowly across the dial, and suddenly he heard a shriek, a frightful piercing shriek, and he jumped and dropped his hands, catching hold of the edge of the table. He stared around him as if expecting to see the person who had shrieked. There was no one in sight except the woman in the garden next door, and it was certainly not she. She was bending down, cutting yellow roses and putting them in her basket.

Again it came—a throatless, inhuman shriek, sharp and short, very clear and cold. The note itself possessed a minor, metallic quality that he had never heard before. Klausner looked around him, searching instinctively for the source of the noise. The woman next door was the only living thing in sight. He saw her reach down, take a rose stem in the fingers of one hand, and snip the stem with a pair of scissors. Again he heard the scream.

It came at the exact moment when the rose stem was cut.

At this point, the woman straightened up, put the scissors in the basket with the roses and turned to walk away.

"Mrs. Saunders!" Klausner shouted, his voice shrill with excitement. "Oh, Mrs. Saunders!"

And looking round, the woman saw her neighbor standing on his lawn—a fantastic, arm-waving little person with a pair of earphones on his head—calling to her in a voice so high and loud that she became alarmed.

"Cut another one! Please cut another one quickly!"

She stood still, staring at him. "Why, Mr. Klausner," she said. "What's the matter?"

"Please do as I ask," he said. "Cut just one more rose!"

Mrs. Saunders had always believed her neighbor to be a rather peculiar person; now it seemed that he had gone completely crazy. She wondered whether she should run into the house and fetch her husband. No, she thought. No, he's harmless. I'll just humor him. "Certainly, Mr. Klausner, if you like," she said. She took her scissors from the basket, bent down and snipped another rose.

Again Klausner heard that frightful, throatless shriek in the earphones; again it came at the exact moment the rose stem was cut. He took off the earphones and ran to the fence that separated the two gardens. "All right," he said. "That's enough. No more. Please, no more."

The woman stood there, a yellow rose in one hand, clippers in the other, looking at him.

"I'm going to tell you something, Mrs. Saunders," he said, "something that you won't believe." He put his hands on top of the fence and peered at her intently through his thick spectacles. "You have, this evening, cut a basketful of roses. You have with a sharp pair of scissors cut through the stems of living things, and each rose that you cut screamed in the most terrible way. Did you know that, Mrs. Saunders?"

"No," she said. "I certainly didn't know that."

"It happens to be true," he said. He was breathing rather rapidly, but he was trying to control his excitement. "I heard them shrieking.

Each time you cut one, I heard the cry of pain. A very high-pitched sound, approximately one hundred and thirty-two thousand vibrations a second. You couldn't possibly have heard it yourself. But *I* heard it."

"Did you really, Mr. Klausner?" She decided she would make a dash for the house in about five seconds.

"You might say," he went on, "that a rose bush has no nervous system to feel with, no throat to cry with. You'd be right. It hasn't. Not like ours, anyway. But *how do you know, Mrs. Saunders*"—and here he leaned far over the fence and spoke in a fierce whisper—"*how do you know* that a rose bush doesn't feel as much pain when someone cuts its stem in two as you would feel if someone cut your wrist off with a garden shears? *How do you know that?* It's *alive*, isn't it?"

"Yes, Mr. Klausner. Oh yes—and good night." Quickly she turned and ran up the garden to her house. Klausner went back to the table. He put on the earphones and stood for a while listening. He could still hear the faint crackling sound and the humming noise of the machine, but nothing more. He bent down and took hold of a small white daisy growing on the lawn. He took it between thumb and forefinger and slowly pulled it upward and sideways until the stem broke.

From the moment that he started pulling to the moment when the stem broke, he heard—he distinctly heard in the earphones—a faint high-pitched cry, curiously inanimate. He took another daisy and did it again. Once more he heard the cry, but he wasn't sure now that it expressed *pain*. No, it wasn't pain; it was surprise. Or was it? It didn't really express any of the feelings or emotions known to a human being. It was just a cry, a neutral stony cry—a single emotionless note, expressing nothing. It had been the same with the roses. He had been wrong in calling it a cry of pain. A flower probably didn't feel pain. It felt something else which we didn't know about—something called toin or spurl or plinuckment, or anything you like.

He stood up and removed the earphones. It was getting dark and he could see pricks of light shining in the windows of the houses all around him. Carefully he picked up the black box from the table, carried it into the shed and put it on the workbench. Then he went out, locked the door behind him and walked up to the house.

The next morning Klausner was up as soon as it was light. He dressed and went straight to the shed. He picked up the machine and carried it outside, clasping it to his chest with both hands, walking unsteadily under its weight. He went past the house, out through the front gate, and across the road to the park. There he paused and looked around him; then he went on until he came to a large tree, a beech tree, and he placed the machine on the ground close to the trunk of the tree. Quickly he went back to the house and got an ax from the coal cellar and carried it across the road into the park. He put the axe on the ground beside the tree. Then he looked around him again, peering nervously through his thick glasses in every direction. There was no one about. It was six in the morning.

He put the earphones on his head and switched on the machine. He listened for a moment to the faint familiar humming sound; then he picked up the ax, took a stance with his legs wide apart and swung the ax as hard as he could at the base of the tree trunk. The blade cut deep into the wood and stuck there, and at the instant of impact he heard a most extraordinary noise in the earphones. It was a new noise, unlike any he had heard before—a harsh, noteless, enormous noise, a growling, low-pitched, screaming sound, not quick and short like the noise of the roses, but drawn out like a sob lasting for fully a minute, loudest at the moment when the ax struck, fading gradually fainter and fainter until it was gone.

Klausner stared in horror at the place where the blade of the ax had sunk into the woodflesh of the tree; then gently he took the ax handle, worked the blade loose and threw the thing to the ground. With his fingers he touched the gash that the ax had made in the wood, touching the edges of the gash, trying to press them together to close the wound, and he kept saying, "Tree . . . oh, tree . . . I am sorry . . . I am sorry . . . but it will heal . . . it will heal fine . . ."

For a while he stood there with his hands upon the trunk of the great tree; then suddenly he turned away and hurried off out of the park, across the road, through the front gate and back into his house. He went to the telephone, consulted the book, dialed a number, and waited. He held the receiver tightly in his left hand and tapped the table impatiently with his right. He heard the telephone buzzing at the other end, and then the click of a lifted receiver and a man's voice, a sleepy voice, saying: "Hullo. Yes."

"Dr. Scott?" he said.

"Yes. Speaking."

"Dr. Scott. You must come at once—quickly, please."

"Who is it speaking?"

"Klausner here, and you remember what I told you last night about my experience with sound, and how I hoped I might—"

"Yes, yes, of course, but what's the matter? Are you ill?"

"No, I'm not ill, but—"

"It's half-past six in the morning," the doctor said, "and you call me but you are not ill."

"Please come. Come quickly. I want someone to hear it. It's driving me mad! I can't believe it . . ."

The doctor heard the frantic, almost hysterical note in the man's voice, the same note he was used to hearing in the voices of people who called up and said, "There's been an accident. Come quickly." He said slowly, "You really want me to get out of bed and come over now?"

"Yes, now. At once, please."

"All right, then—I'll come."

Klausner sat down beside the telephone and waited. He tried to remember what the shriek of the tree had sounded like, but he couldn't. He could remember only that it had been enormous and frightful and that it had made him feel sick with horror. He tried to imagine what sort of noise a human would make if he had to stand anchored to the ground while someone deliberately swung a small sharp thing at his leg so that the blade cut in deep and wedged itself in the cut. Same sort of noise perhaps? No. Quite different. The noise of the tree was worse than any known human noise because of that frightening, toneless, throatless quality. He began to wonder about other living things, and he thought immediately of a field of wheat standing up straight and yellow and alive, with the mower going through it, cutting the stems, five hundred stems a second, every second. Oh, my God, what would *that* noise be like? Five hundred wheat plants screaming together and every second another five hundred being cut and screaming and—no, he thought, I do not want to go to a wheat field with my machine. I would never eat bread after that. But what about potatoes and cabbages and carrots and onions? And what about apples? Ah, no. Apples are all right. They fall off naturally when they are ripe. Apples are all right if you let them fall off instead of tearing them from the tree branch. But not vegetables. Not a potato for example. A potato would surely shriek; so would a carrot and an onion and a cabbage . . .

He heard the click of the front-gate latch and he jumped up and went out and saw the tall doctor coming down the patch, little black bag in hand.

"Well," the doctor said. "Well, what's all the trouble?"

"Come with me, doctor, I want you to hear it. I called you because you're the only one I've told. It's over the road in the park. Will you come now?"

The doctor looked at him. He seemed calmer now. There was no sign of madness or hysteria; he was merely disturbed and excited.

They went across the road into the park and Klausner led the way to the great beech tree at the foot of which stood the long black coffin-box of the machine—and the ax.

"Why did you bring it out here?" the doctor asked.

"I wanted a tree. There aren't any big trees in the garden."

"And why the ax?"

"You'll see in a moment. But now please put on these earphones and listen. Listen carefully and tell me afterwards precisely what you hear. I want to make quite sure . . ."

The doctor smiled and took the earphones and put them over his ears.

Klausner bent down and flicked the switch on the panel of the machine; then he picked up the ax and took his stance with his legs apart, ready to swing. For a moment he paused.

"Can you hear anything?" he said to the doctor.

"Can I what?"

"Can you *hear* anything?"

"Just a humming noise."

Klausner stood there with the ax in his hands trying to bring himself to swing, but the thought of the noise that the tree would make made him pause again.

"What are you waiting for?" the doctor asked.

"Nothing," Klausner answered, and then lifted the ax and swung it at the tree, and as he swung, he thought he felt, he could swear he felt a movement of the ground on which he stood. He felt a slight shifting of the earth beneath his feet as though the roots of the tree were moving underneath the soil, but it was too late to check the blow and the ax blade struck the tree and wedged deep into the wood. At that moment, high overhead, there was the cracking sound of wood splintering and the swishing sound of leaves brushing against other leaves and they both looked up and the doctor cried, "Watch out! Run, man! Quickly, run!"

The doctor had ripped off the earphones and was running away fast, but Klausner stood spellbound, staring up at the great branch, sixty feet long at least, that was bending slowly downward, breaking and crackling and splintering at its thickest point, where it joined the main trunk of the tree. The branch came crashing down and Klausner leapt aside just in time. It fell upon the machine and smashed it into pieces.

"Great heavens!" shouted the doctor as he came running back. "That was a near one! I thought it had got you!"

Klausner was staring at the tree. His large head was leaning to one side and upon his smooth white face there was a tense, horrified expression. Slowly he walked up to the tree and gently he prised the blade loose from the trunk.

"Did you hear it?" he said, turning to the doctor. His voice was barely audible.

The doctor was still out of breath from running and the excitement. "Hear what?"

"In the earphones. Did you hear anything when the ax struck?"

The doctor began to rub the back of his neck. "Well," he said, "as a matter of fact . . ." He paused and frowned and bit his lower lip. "No, I'm not sure. I couldn't be sure. I don't suppose I had the earphones on for more than a second after the ax struck."

"Yes, yes, but what did you hear?"

"I don't know," the doctor said. "I don't know what I heard. Probably the noise of the branch breaking." He was speaking rapidly, rather irritably.

"What did it sound like?" Klausner leaned forward slightly, staring hard at the doctor. "*Exactly* what did it sound like?"

"Oh hell!" the doctor said, "I really don't know. I was more interested in getting out of the way. Let's leave it."

"Dr. Scott, *what-did-it-sound-like?*"

"For God's sake, how could I tell, what with half the tree falling on me and having to run for my life?" The doctor certainly seemed nervous. Klausner had sensed it now. He stood quite still, staring at the doctor and for fully half a minute he didn't speak. The doctor moved his feet, shrugged his shoulders and half turned to go. "Well," he said, "we'd better get back."

"Look," said the little man, and now his smooth white face became suddenly suffused with color. "Look," he said, "you stitch this up." He pointed to the last gash that the ax had made in the tree trunk. "You stitch this up quickly."

"Don't be silly," the doctor said.

"You do as I say. Stitch it up." Klausner was gripping the ax handle and he spoke softly, in a curious, almost a threatening tone.

"Don't be silly," the doctor said. "I can't stitch through wood. Come on. Let's get back."

"So you can't stitch through wood?"

"No, of course not."

"Have you got any iodine in your bag?"

"What if I have?"

"Then paint the cut with iodine. It'll sting, but that can't be helped."

"Now look," the doctor said, and again he turned as if to go. "Let's not be ridiculous. Let's get back to the house and then . . ."

"Paint-the-cut-with-iodine."

The doctor hesitated. He saw Klausner's hands tightening on the handle of the ax. He decided that his only alternative was to run away fast, and he certainly wasn't going to do that.

"All right," he said. "I'll paint it with iodine."

He got his black bag which was lying on the grass about ten yards away, opened it and took out a bottle of iodine and some cotton wool. He went up to the tree trunk, uncorked the bottle, tipped some of the iodine on to the cotton wool, bent down and began to dab it into the cut. He kept one eye on Klausner who was standing motionless with the ax in his hands, watching him.

"Make sure you get it right in."

"Yes," the doctor said.

"Now do the other one—the one just above it!"

The doctor did as he was told.

51

"There you are," he said. "It's done."

He straightened up and surveyed his work in a very serious manner. "That should do nicely."

Klausner came closer and gravely examined the two wounds.

"Yes," he said, nodding his huge head slowly up and down. "Yes, that will do nicely." He stepped back a pace. "You'll come and look at them again tomorrow?"

"Oh, yes," the doctor said. "Of course."

"And put some more iodine on?"

"If necessary, yes."

"Thank you, doctor," Klausner said, and he nodded his head again and he dropped the ax and all at once he smiled, a wild, excited smile, and quickly the doctor went over to him and gently he took him by the arm and he said, "Come on, we must go now," and suddenly they were walking away, the two of them, walking silently, rather hurriedly across the park, over the road, back to the house.

AN AFRICAN STORY

For England, the war began in September 1939. The people on the island knew about it at once and began to prepare themselves. In farther places the people heard about it a few minutes afterwards, and they too began to prepare themselves.

And in East Africa, in Kenya Colony, there was a young man who was a white hunter, who loved the plains and the valleys and the cool nights on the slopes of Kilimanjaro. He too heard about the war and began to prepare himself. He made his way over the country to Nairobi, and he reported to the RAF and asked that they make him a pilot. They took him in and he began his training at Nairobi airport, flying in little Tiger Moths and doing well with his flying.

After five weeks he nearly got court-martialed because he took his plane up and instead of practicing spins and stall-turns as he had been ordered to do, he flew off in the direction of Nakuru to look at the wild animals on the plain. On the way, he thought he saw a sable antelope, and because these are rare animals, he became excited and flew down low to get a better view. He was looking down at the antelope out of the left side of the cockpit, and because of this he did not see the giraffe on the other side. The leading edge of the starboard wing struck the neck of the giraffe just below the head and cut clean through it. He was

53

flying as low as that. There was damage to the wing, but he managed to get back to Nairobi, and as I said, he was nearly court-martialed, because you cannot explain away a thing like that by saying you hit a large bird, not when there are pieces of giraffe skin and giraffe hair sticking to the wing and the stays.

After six weeks he was allowed to make his first solo cross-country flight, and he flew off from Nairobi to a place called Eldoret, which is a little town eight thousand feet up in the Highlands. But again he was unlucky. This time he had engine failure on the way, due to water in the fuel tanks. He kept his head and made a beautiful forced landing without damaging the aircraft, not far from a little shack which stood alone on the highland plain with no other habitation in sight. That is lonely country up there.

He walked over to the shack, and there he found an old man, living alone, with nothing but a small patch of sweet potatoes, some brown chickens, and a black cow.

The old man was kind to him. He gave him food and milk and a place to sleep, and the pilot stayed with him for two days and two nights, until a rescue plane from Nairobi spotted his aircraft on the ground, landed beside it, found out what was wrong, went away and came back with clean petrol which enabled him to take off and return.

But during his stay, the old man, who was lonely and had seen no one for many months, was glad of his company and of the opportunity to talk. He talked much and the pilot listened. He talked of the lonely life, of the lions that came in the night, of the rogue elephant that lived over the hill in the west, of the hotness of the days and of the silence that came with the cold at midnight.

On the second night he talked about himself. He told a long, strange story, and as he told it, it seemed to the pilot that the old man was lifting a great weight off his shoulders in the telling. When he had finished, he said that he had never told that to anyone before, and that he would never tell it to anyone again, but the story was so strange that the pilot wrote it down on paper as soon as he got back to Nairobi. He wrote it not in the old man's words but in his own words, painting it as a picture with the old man as a character in the picture, because that was the best way to do it. He had never written a story before, and so naturally there were mistakes. He did not know any of the tricks with words which writers use, which they have to use just as painters have to use tricks with paint, but when he had finished writing, when he put down his pencil and went over to the airmen's canteen for a pint of beer, he left behind him a rare and powerful tale.

We found it in his suitcase two weeks later when we were going through his belongings after he had been killed in training, and because he seemed to have no relatives, and because he was my friend, I took the manuscript and looked after it for him.

This is what he wrote.

The old man came out of the door into the bright sunshine, and for a moment he stood leaning on his stick, looking around him, blinking at the strong light. He stood with his head on one side, looking up, listening for the noise which he thought he had heard.

He was small and thick and well over seventy years old, although he looked nearer eighty-five, because rheumatism had tied his body into knots. His face was covered with gray hair, and when he moved his mouth, he moved it only on one side of his face. On his head, whether indoors or out, he wore a dirty white topee.

He stood quite still in the bright sunshine, screwing up his eyes, listening for the noise.

Yes, there it was again. The head of the old man flicked around and he looked towards the small wooden hut standing a hundred yards away on the pasture. This time there was no doubt about it: the yelp of a dog, the high-pitched, sharp-piercing yelp of pain which a dog gives when he is in great danger. Twice more it came and this time the noise was more like a scream than a yelp. The note was higher and more sharp, as though it were wrenched quickly from some small place inside the body.

The old man turned and limped fast across the grass towards the wooden shed where Judson lived, pushed open the door and went in.

The small white dog was lying on the floor and Judson was standing over it, his legs apart, his black hair falling all over his long, red face; standing there tall and skinny, muttering to himself and sweating through his greasy white shirt. His mouth hung open in an odd, lifeless way, as though his jaw was too heavy for him, and he was dribbling gently down the middle of his chin. He stood there looking at the small white dog which was lying on the floor, and with one hand he was slowly twisting his left ear; in the other he held a heavy bamboo.

The old man ignored Judson and went down on his knees beside his dog, gently running his thin hands over its body. The dog lay still, looking up at him with watery eyes. Judson did not move. He was watching the dog and the man.

Slowly the old man got up, rising with difficulty, holding the top of his stick with both hands and pulling himself to his feet. He looked around the room. There was a dirty rumpled mattress lying on the floor in the far corner; there was a wooden table made of packing cases and on it a Primus stove and a chipped blue-enameled saucepan. There were chicken feathers and mud on the floor.

The old man saw what he wanted. It was a heavy iron bar standing against the wall near the mattress, and he hobbled over towards it, thumping the hollow wooden floorboards with his stick as he went. The eyes of the dog followed his movements as he limped across the room. The old man changed his stick to his left hand, took the iron bar in his right, hobbled back to the dog and without pausing, he lifted the bar and brought it down hard upon the animal's head. He threw the bar to the ground and looked up at Judson, who was standing there with his legs apart, dribbling down his chin and twitching around the corners of his eyes. He went right up to him and began to speak. He spoke very quietly and slowly, with a terrible anger, and as he spoke he moved only one side of his mouth.

"You killed him," he said. "You broke his back."

Then, as the tide of anger rose and gave him strength, he found more words. He looked up and spat them into the face of the tall Judson, who twitched around the corners of his eyes and backed away towards the wall.

"You lousy, mean, dog-beating bastard. That was my dog. What the hell right have you got beating my dog, tell me that. Answer me, you slobbering madman. Answer me."

Judson was slowly rubbing the palm of his left hand up and down on the front of his shirt, and now the whole of his face began to twitch. Without looking up, he said, "He wouldn't stop licking that old place on his paw. I couldn't stand the noise it made. You know I can't stand noises like that, licking, licking, licking. I told him to stop. He looked up and wagged his tail; but then he went on licking. I couldn't stand it any longer, so I beat him."

The old man did not say anything. For a moment it looked as though he were going to hit this creature. He half raised his arm, dropped it again, spat on the floor, turned around and hobbled out of the door into the sunshine. He went across the grass to where a black cow was standing in the shade of a small acacia tree, chewing its cud, and the cow watched him as he came limping across the grass from the shed. But it went on chewing, munching its cud, moving its jaws regularly, mechanically, like a metronome in slow time. The old man came limping up and stood beside it, stroking its neck. Then he leant against its shoulder and scratched its back with the butt end of his stick. He stood there for a long time, leaning against the cow, scratching it with his stick; and now and again he would speak to it, speaking quiet little words, whispering them almost, like a person telling a secret to another.

It was shady under the acacia tree, and the country around him looked lush and pleasant after the long rains, for the grass grows green up in the Highlands of Kenya; and at this time of the year, after the rains, it is as green and rich as any grass in the world. Away in the north stood Mount Kenya itself, with snow upon its head, with a thin white plume trailing from its summit where the city winds made a storm and blew the white powder from the top of the mountain. Down below, upon the slopes of that same mountain there were lion and elephant, and sometimes during the night one could hear the roar of the lions as they looked at the moon.

The days passed and Judson went about his work on the farm in a silent, mechanical kind of way, taking in the corn, digging the sweet potatoes and milking the black cow, while the old man stayed indoors away from the fierce African sun. Only in the late afternoon when the air began to get cool and sharp, did he hobble outside, and always he went over to his black cow and spent an hour with it under the acacia tree. One day when he came out he found Judson standing beside the cow, regarding it strangely, standing in a peculiar attitude with one foot in front of the other and gently twisting his ear with his right hand.

"What is it now?" said the old man as he came limping up.

"Cow won't stop chewing," said Judson.

"Chewing her cud," said the old man. "Leave her alone."

Judson said, "It's the noise, can't you hear it? Crunchy noise like she was chewing pebbles, only she isn't; she's chewing grass and spit. Look at her, she goes on and on crunching, crunching, crunching, and it's just grass and spit. Noise goes right into my head."

"Get out," said the old man. "Get out of my sight."

At dawn the old man sat, as he always did, looking out of his window, watching Judson coming across from his hut to milk the cow. He saw him coming sleepily across the field, talking to himself as he walked, dragging his feet, making a dark green trail in the wet grass, carrying in his hand the old four-gallon kerosene tin which he used as a milk pail. The sun was coming up over the escarpment and making long shadows behind the man, the cow and the little acacia tree. The old man saw Judson put down the tin and he saw him fetch the box from beside the acacia tree and settle himself upon it, ready for the milking. He saw him suddenly kneeling down, feeling the udder of the cow with his hands and at the same time the old man noticed from where he sat that the animal had no milk. He saw Judson get up and come walking fast towards the shack. He came and stood under the window where the old man was sitting and looked up.

"Cow's got no milk," he said.

The old man leaned through the open window, placing both his hands on the sill.

"You lousy bastard, you've stole it."

"I didn't take it," said Judson. "I bin asleep."

"You stole it." The old man was leaning farther out of the window, speaking quietly with one side of his mouth. "I'll beat the hell out of you for this," he said.

Judson said, "Someone stole it in the night, a native, one of the Kikuyu. Or maybe she's sick."

It seemed to the old man that he was telling the truth. "We'll see," he said, "if she milks this evening; and now for Christ's sake, get out of my sight."

By evening the cow had a full udder and the old man watched Judson draw two quarts of good thick milk from under her.

The next morning she was empty. In the evening she was full. On the third morning she was empty once more.

On the third night the old man went on watch. As soon as it began to get dark, he stationed himself at the open window with an old twelve-bore shotgun lying on his lap, waiting for the thief who came and milked his cow in the night. At first it was pitch dark and he could not see the cow even, but soon a three-quarter moon came over the hills and it became light, almost as though it was day time. But it was bitter cold because the Highlands are seven thousand feet up, and the old man shivered at his post and pulled his brown blanket closer around his shoulders. He could see the cow well now, just as well as in daylight, and the little acacia tree threw a deep shadow across the grass, for the moon was behind it.

All through the night the old man sat there watching the cow, and save when he got up once and hobbled back into the room to fetch another blanket, his eyes never left her. The cow stood placidly under the small tree, chewing her cud and gazing at the moon.

An hour before dawn her udder was full. The old man could see it; he had been watching it the whole time, and although he had not seen the movement of its swelling any more than one can see the movement of the hour hand of a watch, yet all the time he had been conscious of the filling as the milk came down. It was an hour before dawn. The moon was low, but the light had not gone. He could see the cow and the little tree and the greenness of the grass around the cow. Suddenly he jerked his head. He heard something. Surely that was a noise he heard. Yes, there it was again, a rustling in the grass right underneath the window where he was sitting. Quickly he pulled himself up and looked over the sill onto the ground.

Then he saw it. A large black snake, a Mamba, eight feet long and as thick as a man's arm, was gliding through the wet grass, heading straight for the cow and going fast. Its small pear-shaped head was raised slightly off the ground and the movement of its body against the wetness made a clear hissing sound like gas escaping from a jet. He raised his gun to shoot. Almost at once he lowered it again, why he did not know, and he sat there not moving, watching the Mamba as it approached the cow, listening to the noise it made as it went, watching it come up close to the cow and waiting for it to strike.

But it did not strike. It lifted its head and for a moment let it sway gently back and forth; then it raised the front part of its black body into the air under the udder of the cow, gently took one of the thick teats into its mouth and began to drink.

The cow did not move. There was no noise anywhere, and the body of the Mamba curved gracefully up from the ground and hung under the udder of the cow. Black snake and black cow were clearly visible out there in the moonlight.

For half an hour the old man watched the Mamba taking the milk of the cow. He saw the gentle pulsing of its black body as it drew the liquid out of the udder and he saw it, after a time, change from one teat to another, until at last there was no longer any milk left. Then the Mamba gently lowered itself to the ground and slid back through the grass in the direction whence it came. Once more it made a clear hissing noise as it went, and once more it passed underneath the window where the old man sat, leaving a thin dark trail in the wet grass where it had gone. Then it disappeared behind the shack.

Slowly the moon went down behind the ridge of Mount Kenya. Almost at the same time the sun rose up out of the escarpment in the east and Judson came out of his hut with the four-gallon kerosene tin in his hand, walking sleepily towards the cow, dragging his feet in the heavy dew as he went. The old man watched him coming and waited. Judson bent down and felt the udder with his hand and as he did so, the old man shouted at him. Judson jumped at the sound of the old man's voice.

"It's gone again," said the old man.

Judson said, "Yes, cow's empty."

"I think," said the old man slowly, "I think that it was a Kikuyu boy. I was dozing a bit and only woke up as he was making off. I couldn't shoot because the cow was in the way. He made off behind the cow. I'll wait for him tonight. I'll get him tonight," he added.

Judson did not answer. He picked up his four-gallon tin and walked back to his hut.

That night the old man sat up again by the window watching the cow. For him there was this time a certain pleasure in the anticipation of what he was going to see. He knew that he would see the Mamba again, but he wanted to make quite certain. And so, when the great black snake slid across the grass towards the cow an hour before sunrise, the old man leaned over the windowsill and followed the movements of the Mamba as it approached the cow. He saw it wait for a moment under the belly of the animal, letting its head sway slowly backwards and forwards half a dozen times before finally raising its body from the ground to take the teat of the cow into its mouth. He saw it drink the milk for half an hour, until there was none left, and he saw it lower its body and slide smoothly back behind the shack whence it came. And while he watched these things, the old man began laughing quietly with one side of his mouth.

Then the sun rose up from behind the hills, and Judson came out of his hut with the four-gallon tin in his hand, but this time he went straight to the window of the shack where the old man was sitting wrapped up in his blankets.

"What happened?" said Judson.

The old man looked down at him from his window. "Nothing," he said. "Nothing happened. I dozed off again and the bastard came and took it while I was asleep. Listen, Judson," he added, "we got to catch this boy, otherwise you'll be going short of milk, not that that would do you any harm. But we got to catch him. I can't shoot because he's too clever; the cow's always in the way. You'll have to get him."

"Me get him? How?"

The old man spoke very slowly. "I think," he said, "I think you must hide beside the cow, right beside the cow. That is the only way you can catch him."

Judson was rumpling his hair with his left hand.

"Today," continued the old man, "you will dig a shallow trench right beside the cow. If you lie in it and if I cover you over with hay and grass, the thief won't notice you until he's right alongside."

"He may have a knife," Judson said.

"No, he won't have a knife. You take your stick. That's all you'll need."

Judson said, "Yes, I'll take my stick. When he comes, I'll jump up and beat him with my stick." Then suddenly he seemed to remember something. "What about her chewing?" he said. "Couldn't stand her chewing all night, crunching and crunching, crunching spit and grass like it was pebbles. Couldn't stand that all night," and he began twisting again at his left ear with his hand.

"You'll do as you're bloody well told," said the old man.

That day Judson dug his trench beside the cow which was to be tethered to the small acacia tree so that she could not wander about the field. Then, as evening came and as he was preparing to lie down in the trench for the night, the old man came to the door of his shack and said, "No point in doing anything until early morning. They won't come till the cow's full. Come in here and wait; it's warmer than your filthy little hut."

Judson had never been invited into the old man's shack before. He followed him in, happy that he would not have to lie all night in the trench. There was a candle burning in the room. It was stuck into the neck of a beer bottle and the bottle was on the table.

"Make some tea," said the old man, pointing to the Primus stove standing on the floor. Judson lit the stove and made tea. The two of them sat down on a couple of wooden boxes and began to drink. The old man drank his hot and made loud sucking noises as he drank. Judson kept blowing on his, sipping it cautiously and watching the old man over the top of his cup. The old man went on sucking away at his tea until suddenly Judson said, "Stop." He said it quietly, plaintively almost, and as he said it he began to twitch around the corners of his eyes and around his mouth.

"What?" said the old man.

Judson said, "That noise, that sucking noise you're making."

The old man put down his cup and regarded the other quietly for a few moments, then he said, "How many dogs you killed in your time, Judson?"

There was no answer.

"I said how many? How many dogs?"

Judson began picking the tea leaves out of his cup and sticking them on to the back of his left hand. The old man was leaning forward on his box.

"How many dogs, Judson?"

Judson began to hurry with his tea leaves. He jabbed his fingers into his empty cup, picked out a tea leaf, pressed it quickly onto the back of his hand and quickly went back for another. When there were not many left and he did not find one immediately, he bent over and peered closely into the cup, trying to find the ones that remained. The back of the hand which held the cup was covered with wet black tea leaves.

"Judson!" the old man shouted, and one side of his mouth opened and shut like a pair of tongs. The candle flame flickered and became still again.

Then quietly and very slowly, coaxingly, as someone to a child, "In all your life, how many dogs has it been?"

Judson said, "Why should I tell you?" He did not look up. He was picking the tea leaves off the back of his hand one by one and returning them to the cup.

"I want to know, Judson." The old man was speaking very gently. "I'm getting keen about this too. Let's talk about it and make some plans for more fun."

Judson looked up. A ball of saliva rolled down his chin, hung for a moment in the air, snapped and fell to the floor.

"I only kill 'em because of a noise."

"How often've you done it? I'd love to know how often."

"Lots of times long ago."

"How? Tell me how you used to do it. What did you like best?"

No answer.

"Tell me, Judson. I'd love to know."

"I don't see why I should. It's a secret."

"I won't tell. I swear I won't tell."

"Well, if you'll promise." Judson shifted his seat closer and spoke in a whisper. "Once I waited till one was sleeping, then I got a big stone and dropped it on his head."

The old man got up and poured himself a cup of tea. "You didn't kill mine like that."

"I didn't have time. The noise was so bad, the licking, and I just had to do it quick."

"You didn't even kill him."

"I stopped the noise."

The old man went over to the door and looked out. It was dark. The moon had not yet risen, but the night was clear and cold with many stars. In the east there was a little paleness in the sky, and as he watched, the paleness grew and it changed from a paleness into a brightness, spreading over the sky so that the light was reflected and held by the small drops of dew upon the grass along the highlands; and slowly, the moon rose up over the hills. The old man turned and said, "Better get ready. Never know; they might come early tonight."

Judson got up and the two of them went outside. Judson lay down in the shallow trench beside the cow and the old man covered him over with grass, so that only his head peeped out above the ground. "I shall be watching, too," he said, "from the window. If I give a shout, jump up and catch him."

He hobbled back to the shack, went upstairs, wrapped himself in blankets and took up his position by the window. It was early still. The moon was nearly full and it was climbing. It shone upon the snow on the summit of Mount Kenya.

After an hour the old man shouted out of the window:

"Are you still awake, Judson?"

"Yes," he answered, "I'm awake."

"Don't go to sleep," said the old man. "Whatever you do, don't go to sleep."

"Cow's crunching all the time," said Judson.

"Good, and I'll shoot you if you get up now," said the old man.

"You'll shoot me?"

"I said I'll shoot you if you get up now."

A gentle sobbing noise came up from where Judson lay, a strange gasping sound as though a child was trying not to cry, and in the middle of it, Judson's voice, "I've got to move; please let me move. This crunching."

"If you get up," said the old man. "I'll shoot you in the belly."

For another hour or so the sobbing continued, then quite suddenly it stopped.

Just before four o'clock it began to get very cold and the old man huddled deeper into his blankets and shouted, "Are you cold out there, Judson? Are you cold?"

"Yes," came the answer. "So cold. But I don't mind because cow's not crunching any more. She's asleep."

The old man said, "What are you going to do with the thief when you catch him?"

"I don't know."

"Will you kill him?"

A pause.

"I don't know. I'll just go for him."

"I'll watch," said the old man. "It ought to be fun." He was leaning out of the window with his arms resting on the sill.

Then he heard the hiss under the windowsill, and looked over and saw the black Mamba, sliding through the grass towards the cow, going fast and holding its head just a little above the ground as it went.

When the Mamba was five yards away, the old man shouted. He cupped his hands to his mouth and shouted, "Here he comes, Judson; here he comes. Go and get him."

Judson lifted his head quickly and looked up. As he did so he saw the Mamba and the Mamba saw him. There was a second, or perhaps two, when the snake stopped, drew back and raised the front part of its body in the air. Then the stroke. Just a flash of black and a slight thump as it took him in the chest. Judson screamed, a long, high-pitched scream which did not rise nor fall, but held its note until gradually it faded into nothingness and there was silence. Now he was standing up, ripping open his shirt, feeling for the place in his chest, whimpering quietly, moaning and breathing hard with his mouth wide open. And all the while the old man sat quietly at the open window, leaning forward and never taking his eyes away from the one below.

Everything comes very quick when one is bitten by a black Mamba, and almost at once the poison began to work. It threw him to the ground, where he lay humping his back and rolling around on the grass. He no longer made any noise. It was all very quiet, as though a man of great strength was wrestling with a giant whom one could not see, and it was as though the giant was twisting him and not letting him get up, stretching his arms through the fork of his legs and pushing his knees up under his chin.

Then he began pulling up the grass with his hands and soon after that he lay on his back kicking gently with his legs. But he didn't last very long. He gave a quick wriggle, humped his back again, turning over as he did it, then he lay on the ground quite still, lying on his stomach with his right knee drawn up underneath his chest and his hands stretched out above his head.

Still the old man sat by the window, and even after it was all over, he stayed where he was and did not stir. There was a movement in the shadow under the acacia tree and the Mamba came forward slowly towards the cow. It came forward a little, stopped, raised its head, waited, lowered its head, and slid forward again right under the belly of the animal. It raised itself into the air and took one of the brown teats in its mouth and began to drink. The old man sat watching the Mamba taking the milk of the cow, and once again he saw the gentle pulsing of its body as it drew the liquid out of the udder.

While the snake was still drinking, the old man got up and moved away from the window.

"You can have his share," he said quietly. "We don't mind you having his share," and as he spoke he glanced back and saw again the black body of the Mamba curving upward from the ground, joining with the belly of the cow.

"Yes," he said again, "we don't mind your having his share."

Galloping Foxley

Five days a week, for thirty-six years, I have traveled the eight-twelve train to the City. It is never unduly crowded, and it takes me right into Cannon Street Station, only an eleven and a half minute walk from the door of my office in Austin Friars.

I have always liked the process of commuting; every phase of the little journey is a pleasure to me. There is a regularity about it that is agreeable and comforting to a person of habit, and in addition, it serves as a sort of slipway along which I am gently but firmly launched into the waters of daily business routine.

Ours is a smallish country station and only nineteen or twenty people gather there to catch the eight-twelve. We are a group that rarely changes, and when occasionally a new face appears on the platform it causes a certain disclamatory, protestant ripple, like a new bird in a cage of canaries.

But normally, when I arrive in the morning with my usual four minutes to spare, there they all are, good, solid, steadfast people, standing in their right places with their right umbrellas and hats and ties and faces and their newspapers under their arms, as unchanged and unchangeable through the years as the furniture in my own living room. I like that.

I like also my corner seat by the window and reading *The Times* to the noise and motion of the train. This part of it lasts thirty-two minutes and it seems to soothe both my brain and my fretful old body like a good long massage. Believe me, there's nothing like routine and regularity for preserving one's peace of mind. I have now made this morning journey nearly ten thousand times in all, and I enjoy it more and more every day. Also (irrelevant, but interesting), I have become a sort of clock. I can tell at once if we are running two, three, or four minutes late, and I never have to look up to know which station we are stopped at.

The walk at the other end from Cannon Street to my office is neither too long nor too short—a healthy little perambulation along streets crowded with fellow commuters all proceeding to their places of work on the same orderly schedule as myself. It gives me a sense of assurance to be moving among these dependable, dignified people who stick to their jobs and don't go gadding about all over the world. Their lives, like my own, are regulated nicely by the minute hand of an accurate watch, and very often our paths cross at the same times and places on the street each day.

For example, as I turn the corner into St. Swithin's Lane, I invariably come head on with a genteel middle-aged lady who wears silver pince-nez and carries a black briefcase in her hand—a first-rate accountant, I should say, or possibly an executive in the textile industry. When I cross over Threadneedle Street by the traffic lights, nine times out of ten I pass a gentleman who wears a different garden flower in his buttonhole each day. He dresses in black trousers and gray spats and is clearly a punctual and meticulous person, probably a banker, or perhaps a solicitor like myself; and several times in the last twenty-five years, as we have hurried past one another across the street, our eyes have met in a fleeting glance of mutual approval and respect.

At least half the faces I pass on this little walk are now familiar to me. And good faces they are too, my kind of faces, my kind of people—sound, sedulous, businesslike folk with none of that restlessness and glittering eye about them that you see in all these so-called clever types who want to tip the world upside-down with their Labor Governments and socialized medicines and all the rest of it.

So you can see that I am, in every sense of the words, a contented commuter. Or would it be more accurate to say that I *was* a contented commuter? At the time when I wrote the little autobiographical sketch you have just read—intending to circulate it among the staff of my office as an exhortation and an example—I was giving a perfectly true account of my feelings. But that was a whole week ago, and since then something rather peculiar has happened. As a matter of fact, it started to happen last Tuesday, the very morning that I was carrying the rough draft up to Town in my pocket; and this, to me, was so timely and coincidental that I can only believe it to have been the work of God. God had read my little essay and he had said to himself, "This man Perkins is becoming over-complacent. It is high time I taught him a lesson." I honestly believe that's what happened.

As I say, it was last Tuesday, the Tuesday after Easter, a warm yellow spring morning, and I was striding on to the platform of our small country station with *The Times* tucked under my arm and the draft of "The Contented Commuter" in my pocket, when I immediately became aware that something was wrong. I could actually *feel* that curious little ripple of protest running along the ranks of my fellow commuters. I stopped and glanced around.

The stranger was standing plumb in the middle of the platform, feet apart and arms folded, looking for all the world as though he owned the whole place. He was a biggish, thickset man, and even from behind he somehow managed to convey a powerful impression of arrogance and oil. Very definitely, he was not one of us. He carried a cane instead of an umbrella, his shoes were brown instead of black, the gray hat was cocked at a ridiculous angle, and in one way and another there seemed to be an excess of silk and polish about his person. More than this I did not care to observe. I walked straight past him with my face to the sky, adding, I sincerely hope, a touch of real frost to an atmosphere that was already cool.

The train came in. And now, try if you can to imagine my horror when the new man actually followed me into *my own* compartment! Nobody had done this to me for fifteen years. My colleagues always respect my seniority. One of my special little pleasures is to have the place to myself for at least one, sometimes two or even three stations. But here, if you please, was this fellow, this stranger, straddling the seat opposite and blowing his nose and rustling the *Daily Mail* and lighting a disgusting pipe.

I lowered my *Times* and stole a glance at his face. I suppose he was about the same age as me—sixty-two or three—but he had one of those unpleasantly handsome, brown, leathery countenances that you see nowadays in advertisements for men's shirts—the lion shooter and the polo player and the Everest climber and the tropical explorer and the racing yatchsman all rolled into one; dark eyebrows, steely eyes, strong white teeth clamping the stem of a pipe. Personally, I mistrust all handsome men. The superficial pleasures of this life come too easily to them, and they seem to walk the world as though they themselves were personally responsible for their own good looks. I don't mind a *woman* being pretty. That's different. But in a man, I'm sorry, but somehow or other I find it downright offensive. Anyway, here was this one sitting right opposite me in the carriage, and I was looking at him over the top of my *Times* when suddenly he glanced up and our eyes met.

"D'you mind the pipe?" he asked, holding it up in his fingers. That was all he said. But the sound of his voice had a sudden and extraordinary effect upon me. In fact, I think I jumped. Then I sort of froze up and sat staring at him for at least a minute before I got hold of myself and made an answer.

"This is a smoker," I said, "so you may do as you please."

"I just thought I'd ask."

There it was again, that curiously crisp, familiar voice, clipping its words and spitting them out very hard and small like a little quick-firing gun shooting out raspberry seeds. Where had I heard it before, and why did every word seem to strike upon some tiny tender spot far back in my memory? Good heavens, I thought. Pull yourself together. What sort of nonsense is this?

The stranger returned to his paper. I pretended to do the same. But by this time I was properly put out and I couldn't concentrate at all. Instead, I kept stealing glances at him over the top of the editorial page. It was really an intolerable face, vulgarly, almost lasciviously handsome, with an oily salacious sheen all over the skin. But had I or had I not seen it before some time in my life? I began to think I had, because

75

now, even when I looked at it I felt a peculiar kind of discomfort that I cannot quite describe—something to do with pain and with violence, perhaps even with fear.

We spoke no more during the journey, but you can well imagine that by then my whole routine had been thoroughly upset. My day was ruined; and more than one of my clerks at the office felt the sharper edge of my tongue, particularly after luncheon when my digestion started acting up on me as well.

The next morning, there he was again standing in the middle of the platform with his cane and his pipe and his silk scarf and his nauseatingly handsome face. I walked past him and approached a certain Mr. Grummitt, a stockbroker who has been commuting with me for over twenty-eight years. I can't say I've ever had an actual conversation with him before—we are rather a reserved lot on our station—but a crisis like this will usually break the ice.

"Grummitt," I whispered. "Who's this bounder?"

"Search me," Grummitt said.

"Pretty unpleasant."

"Very."

"Not going to be a regular, I trust."

"Oh God," Grummitt said.

Then the train came in.

This time, to my relief, the man got into another compartment.

But the following morning I had him with me again.

"Well," he said, settling back in the seat directly opposite. "It's a *topping* day." And once again I felt that slow uneasy stirring of the memory, stronger than ever this time, closer to the surface but not yet quite within my reach.

Then came Friday, the last day of the week. I remember it had rained as I drove to the station, but it was one of those warm sparkling April showers that last only five or six minutes, and when I walked on to the platform, all the umbrellas were rolled up and the sun was shining and there were big white clouds floating in the sky. In spite of this, I felt depressed. There was no pleasure in this journey for me any longer. I knew the stranger would be there. And sure enough, he was, standing with his legs apart just as though he owned the place, and this time swinging his cane casually back and forth through the air.

The cane! That did it! I stopped like I'd been shot.

"It's Foxley!" I cried under my breath. "Galloping Foxley! And still swinging his cane!"

I stepped closer to get a better look. I tell you I've never had such a shock in all my life. It was Foxley all right. Bruce Foxley or Galloping Foxley as we used to call him. And the last time I'd seen him, let me see—it was at school and I was no more than twelve or thirteen years old.

At that point the train came in, and heaven help me if he didn't get into my compartment once again. He put his hat and cane up on the rack, then turned and sat down and began lighting his pipe. He glanced up at me through the smoke with those rather small cold eyes and he said, "*Ripping* day, isn't it. Just like summer."

There was no mistaking the voice now. It hadn't changed at all. Except that the things I had been used to hearing it say were different.

"All right, Perkins," it used to say. "All right, you nasty little boy. I am about to beat you again."

How long ago was that? It must be nearly fifty years. Extraordinary, though, how little the features had altered. Still the same arrogant tilt of the chin, the flaring nostrils, the contemptuous staring eyes that were too small and a shade too close together for comfort; still the same habit of thrusting his face forward at you, impinging on you pushing you into a corner; and even the hair I could remember—coarse and slightly wavy, with just a trace of oil all over it, like a well-tossed salad. He used to keep a bottle of green hair mixture on the side table in his study—when you have to dust a room you get to know and to hate all the objects in it—and this bottle had the royal coat of arms on the label and the name of a shop in Bond Street, and under that, in small print, it said "By Appointment—Hairdressers to His Majesty King Edward VII." I can remember that particularly because it seemed so funny that a shop should want to boast about being hairdresser to someone who was practically bald—even a monarch.

And now I watched Foxley settle back in his seat and begin reading the paper. It was a curious sensation, sitting only a yard away from this man who fifty years before had made me so miserable that I had once contemplated suicide. He hadn't recognized *me;* there wasn't much danger of that because of my moustache. I felt fairly sure I was safe and could sit there and watch him all I wanted.

Looking back on it, there seems little doubt that I suffered very badly at the hands of Bruce Foxley my first year in school, and strangely enough, the unwitting cause of it all was my father. I was twelve and a half when I first went off to this fine old public school. That was, let me see, in 1907. My father, who wore a silk topper and morning coat, escorted me to the station, and I can remember how we were standing on the platform among piles of wooden tuck boxes and trunks and what seemed like thousands of very large boys milling about and talking and shouting at one another, when suddenly somebody who was wanting to get by us gave my father a great push from behind and nearly knocked him off his feet.

My father, who was a small, courteous, dignified person, turned around with surprising speed and seized the culprit by the wrist.

"Don't they teach you better manners than that at this school, young man?" he said.

The boy, at least a head taller than my father, looked down at him with a cold, arrogant-laughing glare, and said nothing.

"It seems to me," my father said, staring back at him, "that an apology would be in order."

But the boy just kept on looking down his nose at my father with this funny little arrogant smile at the corners of his mouth, and his chin kept coming further and further out.

"You strike me as being an impudent and ill-mannered boy," my father went on. "And I can only pray that you are an exception in your school. I would not wish for any son of mine to pick up such habits."

At this point, the big boy inclined his head slightly in my direction, and a pair of small, cold, rather close together eyes looked down into mine. I was not particularly frightened at the time; I knew nothing about the power of senior boys over junior boys at public schools; and I can remember that I looked straight back at him in support of my father, whom I adored and respected.

When my father started to say something more, the boy simply turned away and sauntered slowly down the platform into the crowd.

Bruce Foxley never forgot this episode; and of course the really unlucky thing about it for me was that when I arrived at school I found myself in the same "house" as him. Even worse than that—I was in his study. He was doing his last year, and he was a prefect—"a boazer" we called it—and as such he was officially permitted to beat any of the fags in the house. But being in his study, I automatically became his own particular, personal slave. I was his valet and cook and maid and errand boy, and it was my duty to see that he never lifted a finger for himself unless absolutely necessary. In no society that I know of in the world is a servant imposed upon to the extent that we wretched little fags were imposed upon by the boazers at school. In frosty or snowy weather I even had to sit on the seat of the lavatory (which was in an unheated outhouse) every morning after breakfast to warm it before Foxley came along.

I could remember how he used to saunter across the room in his loose-jointed, elegant way, and if a chair were in his path he would knock it aside and I would have to run over and pick it up. He wore silk shirts and always had a silk handkerchief tucked up his sleeve, and his shoes were made by someone called Lobb (who also had a royal crest). They were pointed shoes, and it was my duty to rub the leather with a bone for fifteen minutes each day to make it shine.

But the worst memories of all had to do with the changing room.

I could see myself now, a small pale shrimp of a boy standing just inside the door of this huge room in my pajamas and bedroom slippers and brown camel-hair dressing gown. A single bright electric bulb was hanging on a flex from the ceiling, and all around the walls the black and yellow football shirts with their sweaty smell filling the room, and the voice, the clipped, pip-spitting voice was saying, "So which is it to be this time? Six with the dressing gown on—or four with it off?"

I never could bring myself to answer this question. I would simply stand there staring down at the dirty floor planks, dizzy with fear and unable to think of anything except that this other larger boy would soon start smashing away at me with his long, thin, white stick, slowly, scientifically, skillfully, legally, and with apparent relish, and I would bleed. Five hours earlier, I had failed to get the fire to light in his study. I had spent my pocket money on a box of special firelighters and I had held a newspaper across the chimney opening to make a draft and I had knelt down in front of it and blown my guts out into the bottom of the grate; but the coals would not burn.

"If you're too obstinate to answer," the voice was saying, "then I'll have to decide for you."

I wanted desperately to answer because I knew which one I had to choose. It's the first thing you learn when you arrive. Always keep the dressing gown *on* and take the extra strokes. Otherwise you're almost certain to get cut. Even three with it on is better than one with it off.

"Take it off then and get into the far corner and touch your toes. I'm going to give you four."

Slowly I would take it off and lay it on the ledge above the boot lockers. And slowly I would walk over to the far corner, cold and naked now in my cotton pajamas, treading softly and seeing everything around me suddenly very bright and flat and far away, like a magic lantern picture, and very big, and very unreal, and sort of swimming through the water in my eyes.

"Go on and touch your toes. Tighter—much tighter than that."

Then he would walk down to the far end of the changing room and I would be watching him upside down between my legs, and he would disappear through a doorway that led down two steps into what we called "the basin passage." This was a stone-floored corridor with wash-basins along one wall, and beyond it was the bathroom. When Foxley disappeared I knew he was walking down to the far end of the basin passage. Foxley always did that. Then, in the distance, but echoing loud among the basins and the tiles, I would hear the noise of his shoes on the stone floor as he started galloping forward, and through my legs I would see him leaping up the two steps into the changing room and come bounding towards me with his face thrust forward and the cane held high in the air. This was the moment when I shut my eyes and waited for the crack and told myself that whatever happened I must not straighten up.

Anyone who has been properly beaten will tell you that the real pain does not come until about eight or ten seconds after the stroke. The stroke itself is merely a loud crack and a sort of blunt thud against your backside, numbing you completely (I'm told a bullet wound does the same). But later on, oh my heavens, it feels as if someone is laying a red hot poker right across your naked buttocks and it is absolutely impossible to prevent yourself from reaching back and clutching it with your fingers.

Foxley knew all about this time lag, and the slow walk back over a distance that must altogether have been fifteen yards gave each stroke plenty of time to reach the peak of its pain before the next one was delivered.

On the fourth stroke I would invariably straighten up. I couldn't help it. It was an automatic defense reaction from a body that had had as much as it could stand.

"You flinched," Foxley would say. "That one doesn't count. Go on—down you get."

The next time I would remember to grip my ankles.

Afterwards he would watch me as I walked over—very stiff now and holding my backside—to put on my dressing gown, but I would always try to keep turned away from him so he couldn't see my face. And when I went out, it would be, "Hey, you! Come back!"

I was in the passage then, and I would stop and turn and stand in the doorway, waiting.

"Come here. Come on, come back here. Now—haven't you forgotten something?"

All I could think of at that moment was the excruciating burning pain in my behind.

"You strike me as being an impudent and ill-mannered boy," he would say, imitating my father's voice. "Don't they teach you better manners than that at this school?"

"Thank . . . you," I would stammer. "Thank . . . you . . . for the beating."

And then back up the dark stairs to the dormitory and it became much better then because it was all over and the pain was going and the others were clustering round and treating me with a certain rough sympathy born of having gone through the same thing themselves, many times.

"Hey, Perkins, let's have a look."

"How many d'you get?"

"Five, wasn't it? We heard them easily from here."

"Come on, man. Let's see the marks."

I would take down my pajamas and stand there while this group of experts solemnly examined the damage.

"Rather far apart, aren't they? Not quite up to Foxley's usual standard."

"Two of them are close. Actually touching. Look—these two are beauties!"

"That low one was a rotten shot."

"Did he go right down the basin passage to start his run?"

"You got an extra one for flinching, didn't you?"

"By golly, old Foxley's really got it in for *you*, Perkins."

"Bleeding a bit too. Better wash it, you know."

Then the door would open and Foxley would be there, and everyone would scatter and pretend to be doing his teeth or saying his prayers while I was left standing in the center of the room with my pants down.

"What's going on here?" Foxley would say, taking a quick look at his own handiwork. "You—Perkins! Put your pajamas on properly and get to bed."

And that was the end of a day.

Through the week, I never had a moment of time to myself. If Foxley saw me in the study taking up a novel or perhaps opening my stamp album, he would immediately find something for me to do. One of his favorites, especially when it was raining outside, was, "Oh, Perkins, I think a bunch of wild irises would look rather nice on my desk, don't you?"

Wild irises grew only around Orange Ponds. Orange Ponds was two miles down the road and half a mile across the fields. I would get up from my chair, put on my raincoat and my straw hat, take my umbrella—my brolly—and set off on this long and lonely trek. The straw hat had to be worn at all times outdoors, but it was easily destroyed by rain; therefore the brolly was necessary to protect the hat. On the other hand, you can't keep a brolly over your head while scrambling about on a woody bank looking for irises, so to save my hat from ruin I would put in on the ground under my brolly while I searched for flowers. In this way, I caught many colds.

But the most dreaded day was Sunday. Sunday was for cleaning the study, and how well I can remember the terror of those mornings, the frantic dusting and scrubbing, and then the waiting for Foxley to come in to inspect.

"Finished?" he would ask.

"I . . . I think so."

Then he would stroll over to the drawer of his desk and take out a single white glove, fitting it slowly onto his right hand, pushing each finger well home, and I would stand there watching and trembling as he moved around the room running his white-gloved forefinger along the picture tops, the skirting, the shelves, the windowsills, the lamp shades. I never took my eyes off that finger. For me it was an instrument of doom. Nearly always, it managed to discover some tiny crack that I had overlooked or perhaps hadn't even thought about; and when this happened Foxley would turn slowly around, smiling that dangerous little smile that wasn't a smile, holding up the white finger so that I should see for myself the thin smudge of dust that lay along the side of it.

"Well," he would say. "So you're a lazy little boy. Aren't you?"

No answer.

"Aren't you?"

"I thought I dusted it all."

"Are you or are you not a nasty, lazy little boy?"

"Y-yes."

"But your father wouldn't want you to grow up like that, would he? Your father is very particular about manners, is he not?"

No answer.

"I asked you, is your father particular about manners?"

"Perhaps—yes."

"Therefore I will be doing him a favor if I punish you, won't I?"

"I don't know."

"Won't I?"

"Y-yes."

"We will meet later then, after prayers, in the changing room."

The rest of the day would be spent in an agony of waiting for the evening to come.

Oh my goodness, how it was all coming back to me now. Sunday was also letter-writing time. "Dear Mummy and Daddy—thank you very much for your letter. I hope you are both well. I am, except I have got a cold because I got caught in the rain but it will soon be over. Yesterday we played Shrewsbury and beat them 4–2. I watched and Foxley who you know is the head of our house scored one of our goals. Thank you very much for the cake. With love from William."

I usually went to the lavatory to write my letter, or to the boothole, or the bathroom—any place out of Foxley's way. But I had to watch the time. Tea was at four-thirty, and Foxley's toast had to be ready. Every day I had to make toast for Foxley, and on weekdays there were no fires allowed in the studies, so all the fags, each making toast for his own studyholder, would have to crowd around the one small fire in the library, jockeying for position with his toasting fork. Under these conditions, I still had to see that Foxley's toast was (1) very crisp, (2) not burned at all, (3) hot and ready exactly on time. To fail in any one of these requirements was a "beatable offense."

"Hey, you! What's this?"

"It's toast."

"Is this really your idea of toast?"

"Well . . ."

"You're too idle to make it right, aren't you?"

"I try to make it."

"You know what they do to an idle horse, Perkins?"

"No."

"Are you a horse?"

"No."

"Well—anyway, you're an ass—ha, ha—so I think you qualify. I'll be seeing you later."

Oh, the agony of those days. To burn Foxley's toast was a "beatable offense." So was forgetting to take the mud off Foxley's football boots. So was failing to hang up Foxley's football clothes. So was rolling up Foxley's brolly the wrong way round. So was banging the study door when Foxley was working. So was filling Foxley's bath too hot for him. So was not cleaning the buttons properly on Foxley's OTC uniform. So was making those blue metal-polish smudges on the uniform itself. So was failing to shine the *soles* of Foxley's shoes. So was leaving Foxley's study untidy at any time. In fact, so far as Foxley was concerned, I was practically a beatable offense myself.

I glanced out of the window. My goodness, we were nearly there. I must have been dreaming away like this for quite a while, and I hadn't even opened my *Times*. Foxley was still leaning back in the corner seat opposite me reading his *Daily Mail,* and through a cloud of blue smoke from his pipe I could see the top half of his face over the newspaper, the small bright eyes, the corrugated forehead, the wavy, slightly oily hair.

Looking at him now, after all that time, was a peculiar and rather exciting experience. I knew he was no longer dangerous, but the old memories were still there and I didn't feel altogether comfortable in his presence. It was something like being inside the cage with a tame tiger.

What nonsense is this? I asked myself. Don't be so stupid. My heavens, if you wanted to you could go ahead and tell him exactly what you thought of him and he couldn't touch you. Hey—that was an idea!

Except that—well—after all, was it worth it? I was too old for that sort of thing now, and I wasn't sure that I really felt much anger towards him anyway.

So what should I do? I couldn't sit there staring at him like an idiot.

At that point, a little impish fancy began to take a hold of me. What I would like to do, I told myself, would be to lean across and tap him lightly on the knee and tell him who I was. Then I would watch his face. After that, I would begin talking about our schooldays together, making it just loud enough for the other people in the carriage to hear. I would remind him playfully of some of the things he used to do to me, and perhaps even describe the changing room beatings so as to embarrass him a trifle. A bit of teasing and discomfort wouldn't do him any harm. And it would do *me* an awful lot of good.

Suddenly he glanced up and caught me staring at him. It was the second time this had happened, and I noticed a flicker of irritation in his eyes.

All right, I told myself. Here we go. But keep it pleasant and sociable and polite. It'll be much more effective that way, more embarrassing for him.

So I smiled at him and gave him a courteous little nod. Then, raising my voice, I said, "I do hope you'll excuse me. I'd like to introduce myself." I was leaning forward watching him closely so as not to miss the reaction. "My name is Perkins—William Perkins—and I was at Repton in 1907."

The others in the carriage were sitting very still, and I could sense that they were all listening and waiting to see what would happen next.

"I'm glad to meet you," he said, lowering the paper to his lap. "Mine's Fortescue—Jocelyn Fortescue, Eton 1916."

THE WISH

Under the palm of one hand the child became aware of the scab of an old cut on his kneecap. He bent forward to examine it closely. A scab was always a fascinating thing; it presented a special challenge he was never able to resist.

Yes, he thought, I will pick it off, even if it isn't ready, even if the middle of it sticks, even if it hurts like anything.

With a fingernail he began to explore cautiously around the edges of the scab. He got a nail underneath it, and when he raised it, but ever so slightly, it suddenly came off, the whole hard brown scab came off beautifully, leaving an interesting little circle of smooth red skin.

Nice. Very nice indeed. He rubbed the circle and it didn't hurt. He picked up the scab, put it on his thigh and flipped it with a finger so that it flew away and landed on the edge of the carpet, the enormous red and black and yellow carpet that stretched the whole length of the hall from the stairs on which he sat to the front door in the distance. A tremendous carpet. Bigger than the tennis lawn. Much bigger than that. He regarded it gravely, setting his eyes upon it with mild pleasure. He had never really noticed it before, but now, all of a sudden, the colors seemed to brighten mysteriously and spring out at him in a most dazzling way.

You see, he told himself, I know how it is. The red parts of the carpet are red-hot lumps of coal. What I must do is this: I must walk all the way along it to the front door without touching them. If I touch the red I will be burnt. As a matter of fact, I will be burnt up completely. And the black parts of the carpet . . . yes, the black parts are snakes, poisonous snakes, adders mostly, and cobras, thick like tree trunks round the middle, and if I touch one of *them*, I'll be bitten and I'll die before tea time. And if I get across safely, without being burnt and without being bitten, I will be given a puppy for my birthday tomorrow.

He got to his feet and climbed higher up the stairs to obtain a better view of this vast tapestry of color and death. Was it possible? Was there enough yellow? Yellow was the only color he was allowed to walk on. Could it be done? This was not a journey to be undertaken lightly; the risks were far too great for that. The child's face—a fringe of white-gold hair, two large blue eyes, a small pointed chin—peered down anxiously over the banisters. The yellow was a bit thin in places and there were one or two widish gaps, but it did seem to go all the way along to the other end. For someone who had only yesterday triumphantly traveled the whole length of the brick path from the stables to the summerhouse without touching the cracks, this carpet thing should not be too difficult. Except for the snakes. The mere thought of snakes sent a fine electricity of fear running like pins down the backs of his legs and under the soles of his feet.

He came slowly down the stairs and advanced to the edge of the carpet. He extended one small sandaled foot and placed it cautiously upon a patch of yellow. Then he brought the other foot up, and there was just enough room for him to stand with the two feet together. There! He had started! His bright oval face was curiously intent, a shade whiter perhaps than before, and he was holding his arms out sideways to assist his balance. He took another step, lifting his foot high over a patch of black, aiming carefully with his toe for a narrow channel of yellow on the other side. When he had completed the second step he paused to rest, standing very stiff and still. The narrow channel of yellow ran forward unbroken for at least five yards and he advanced gingerly along it, bit by bit, as though walking a tightrope. Where it finally curled off sideways, he had to take another long stride, this time over a vicious-looking mixture of black and red. Halfway across he began to wobble. He waved his arms around wildly, windmill fashion, to keep his balance, and he got across safely and rested again on the other side. He was quite breathless now, and so tense he stood high on his toes all the time, arms out sideways, fists clenched. He was on a big safe island of yellow. There was lots of room on it, he couldn't possibly fall off, and he stood there resting, hesitating, waiting, wishing he could stay forever on this big safe yellow island. But the fear of not getting the puppy compelled him to go on.

Step by step, he edged further ahead, and between each one he paused to decide exactly where he should put his foot. Once, he had a choice of ways, either to left or right, and he chose the left because although it seemed the more difficult, there was not so much black in that direction. The black was what had made him nervous. He glanced quickly over his shoulder to see how far he had come. Nearly halfway. There could be no turning back now. He was in the middle and he couldn't turn back and he couldn't jump off sideways either because it was too far, and when he looked at all the red and all the black that lay ahead of him, he felt that old sudden sickening surge of panic in his chest—like last Easter time, that afternoon when he got lost all alone in the darkest part of Piper's Wood.

He took another step, placing his foot carefully upon the only little piece of yellow within reach, and this time the point of the foot came within a centimeter of some black. It wasn't touching the black, he could see it wasn't touching, he could see the small line of yellow separating the toe of his sandal from the black; but the snake stirred as though sensing his nearness, and raised its head and gazed at the foot with bright beady eyes, watching to see if it was going to touch.

"I'm not touching you! You mustn't bite me! You know I'm not touching you!"

Another snake slid up noiselessly beside the first, raised its head, two heads now, two pairs of eyes staring at the foot, gazing at a little naked place just below the sandal strap where the skin showed through. The child went high up on his toes and stayed there, frozen stiff with terror. It was minutes before he dared to move again.

The next step would have to be a really long one. There was this deep curling river of black that ran clear across the width of the carpet, and he was forced by his position to cross it at its widest part. He thought first of trying to jump it, but decided he couldn't be sure of landing accurately on the narrow band of yellow on the other side. He took a deep breath, lifted one foot, and inch by inch he pushed it out in front of him, far far out, then down and down until at last the tip of his sandal was across and resting safely on the edge of the yellow. He leaned forward, transferring his weight to his front foot. Then he tried to bring the back foot up as well. He strained and pulled and jerked his body, but the legs were too wide apart and he couldn't make it. He tried to get back again. He couldn't do that either. He was doing the splits and he was properly stuck. He glanced down and saw this deep curling river of black underneath him. Parts of it were stirring now, and uncoiling and beginning to shine with a dreadfully oily glister. He wobbled, waved his arms frantically to keep his balance, but that seemed to make it worse. He was starting to go over. He was going over to the right, quite slowly he was going over, then faster and faster, and at the last moment, instinctively he put out a hand to break the fall and the next thing he saw was this bare hand of his going right into the middle of a great glistening mass of black and he gave one piercing cry as it touched.

Outside in the sunshine, far away behind the house, the mother was looking for her son.

THE SURGEON

"You have done extraordinarily well," Robert Sandy said, seating himself behind the desk. "It's altogether a splendid recovery. I don't think there's any need for you to come and see me any more."

The patient finished putting on his clothes and said to the surgeon, "May I speak to you, please, for another moment?"

"Of course you may," Robert Sandy said. "Take a seat."

The man sat down opposite the surgeon and leaned forward, placing his hands, palms downward, on the top of the desk. "I suppose you still refuse to take a fee?" he said.

"I've never taken one yet and I don't propose to change my ways at this time of life," Robert Sandy told him pleasantly. "I work entirely for the National Health Service and they pay me a very fair salary."

Robert Sandy MA, M.CHIR, FRCS, had been at the Radcliffe Infirmary in Oxford for eighteen years and he was now fifty-two years old, with a wife and three grown-up children. Unlike many of his colleagues, he did not hanker after fame and riches. He was basically a simple man utterly devoted to his profession.

It was now seven weeks since his patient, a university undergraduate, had been rushed into Casualty by ambulance after a nasty car accident in the Banbury Road not far from the hospital. He was suffering from massive abdominal injuries and he had lost consciousness. When the call came through from Casualty for an emergency surgeon, Robert Sandy was up in his office having a cup of tea after a fairly arduous morning's work which had included a gall bladder, a prostate, and a total colostomy, but for some reason he happened to be the only general surgeon available at that moment. He took one more sip of his tea, then walked straight back into the operating theater and started scrubbing up all over again.

After three and a half hours on the operating table, the patient was still alive and Robert Sandy had done everything he could to save his life. The next day, to the surgeon's considerable surprise, the man was showing signs that he was going to survive. In addition, his mind was lucid and he was speaking coherently. It was only then, on the morning after the operation, that Robert Sandy began to realize that he had an important person on his hands. Three dignified gentlemen from the Saudi Arabian Embassy, including the ambassador himself, came into the hospital and the first thing they wanted was to call in all manner of celebrated surgeons from Harley Street to advise on the case. The patient, with bottles suspended all round his bed and tubes running into many parts of his body, shook his head and murmured something in Arabic to the ambassador.

"He says he wants only you to look after him," the ambassador said to Robert Sandy.

"You are very welcome to call in anyone else you choose for consultation," Robert Sandy said.

"Not if he doesn't want us to," the ambassador said. "He says you have saved his life and he has absolute faith in you. We must respect his wishes."

The ambassador then told Robert Sandy that his patient was none other than a prince of royal blood. In other words, he was one of the many sons of the present king of Saudi Arabia.

A few days later, when the prince was off the danger list, the embassy tried once again to persuade him to make a change. They wanted him to be moved to a far more luxurious hospital that catered only for private patients, but the prince would have none of it. "I stay here," he said, "with the surgeon who saved my life."

Robert Sandy was touched by the confidence his patient was putting in him, and throughout the long weeks of recovery, he did his best to ensure that this confidence was not misplaced.

And now, in the consulting room, the prince was saying, "I do wish you would allow me to pay you for all you have done, Mr. Sandy." The young man had spent three years at Oxford and he knew very well that in England a surgeon was always addressed as "Mister" and not "Doctor." "Please let me pay you, Mr. Sandy," he said.

Robert Sandy shook his head. "I'm sorry," he answered, "but I still have to say no. It's just a personal rule of mine and I won't break it."

"But dash it all, you saved my life," the prince said, tapping the palms of his hands on the desk.

"I did no more than any other competent surgeon would have done," Robert Sandy said.

The prince took his hands off the desk and clasped them on his lap. "All right, Mr. Sandy, even though you refuse a fee, there is surely no reason why my father should not give you a small present to show his gratitude."

Robert Sandy shrugged his shoulders. Grateful patients quite often gave him a case of whiskey or a dozen bottles of wine and he accepted these things gracefully. He never expected them, but he was awfully pleased when they arrived. It was a nice way of saying thank you.

The prince took from his jacket pocket a small pouch made of black velvet and he pushed it across the desk. "My father," he said, "has asked me to tell you how enormously indebted he is to you for what you have done. He told me that whether you took a fee or not, I was to make sure you accepted this little gift."

Robert Sandy looked suspiciously at the black pouch, but he made no move to take it.

"My father," the prince went on, "said also to tell you that in his eyes my life is without price and that nothing on earth can repay you adequately for having saved it. This is simply a . . . what shall we call it . . . a present for your next birthday. A small birthday present."

"He shouldn't give me anything," Robert Sandy said.

"Look at it, please," the prince said.

Rather gingerly, the surgeon picked up the pouch and loosened the silk thread at the opening. When he tipped it upside down, there was a flash of brilliant light as something ice white dropped on to the plain wooden desk top. The stone was about the size of a cashew nut or a bit larger, perhaps three-quarters of an inch long from end to end, and it was pear shaped, with a very sharp point at the narrow end. Its many facets glimmered and sparkled in the most wonderful way.

"Good gracious me," Robert Sandy said, looking at it but not yet touching it. "What is it?"

"It's a diamond," the prince said. "Pure white. It's not especially large, but the color is good."

"I really can't accept a present like this," Robert Sandy said. "No, it wouldn't be right. It must be quite valuable."

The prince smiled at him. "I must tell you something, Mr. Sandy," he said. "Nobody refuses a gift from the king. It would be a terrible insult. It has never been done."

Robert Sandy looked back at the prince. "Oh dear," he said. "You *are* making it awkward for me, aren't you?"

"It is not awkward at all," the prince said, "Just take it."

"You could give it to the hospital."

"We have already made a donation to the hospital," the prince said. "Please take it, not just for my father, but for me as well."

"You are very kind," Robert Sandy said. "All right, then. But I feel quite embarrassed." He picked up the diamond and placed it in the palm of one hand. "There's never been a diamond in our family before," he said. "Gosh, it is beautiful, isn't it. You must please convey my thanks to His Majesty and tell him I shall always treasure it."

"You don't actually have to hang on to it," the prince said. "My father would not be in the least offended if you were to sell it. Who knows, one day you might need a little pocket money."

"I don't think I shall sell it," Robert Sandy said. "It is too lovely. Perhaps I shall have it made into a pendant for my wife."

"What a nice idea," the prince said, getting up from his chair. "And please remember what I told you before. You and your wife are invited to my country at any time. My father would be happy to welcome you both."

"That's very good of him," Robert Sandy said. "I won't forget."

When the prince had gone, Robert Sandy picked up the diamond again and examined it with total fascination. It was dazzling in its beauty, and as he moved it gently from side to side in his palm, one facet after the other caught the light from the window and flashed brilliantly with blue and pink and gold. He glanced at his watch. It was ten minutes past three. An idea had come to him. He picked up the telephone and asked his secretary if there was anything else urgent for him to do that afternoon. If there wasn't, he told her, then he thought he might leave early.

"There's nothing that can't wait until Monday," the secretary said, sensing that for once this most hardworking of men had some special reason for wanting to go.

"I've got a few things of my own I'd very much like to do."

"Off you go, Mr. Sandy," she said. "Try to get some rest over the weekend. I'll see you on Monday."

In the hospital car park, Robert Sandy unchained his bicycle, mounted, and rode out on to the Woodstock Road. He still bicycled to work every day unless the weather was foul. It kept him in shape and it also meant his wife could have the car. There was nothing odd about that. Half the population of Oxford rode on bicycles. He turned into the Woodstock Road and headed for the High. The only good jeweler in town had his shop in the High, halfway up on the right and he was called H. F. Gold. It said so above the window, and most people knew that H stood for Harry. Harry Gold had been there a long time, but Robert had only been inside once, years ago, to buy a small bracelet for his daughter as a confirmation present.

He parked his bike against the curb outside the shop and went in. A woman behind the counter asked if she could help him.

"Is Mr. Gold in?" Robert Sandy said.

"Yes, he is."

"I would like to see him privately for a few minutes, if I may. My name is Sandy."

"Just a minute, please." The woman disappeared through a door at the back, but in thirty seconds she returned and said, "Will you come this way, please."

Robert Sandy walked into a large untidy office in which a small, oldish man was seated behind a partner's desk. He wore a gray goatee beard and steel spectacles, and he stood up as Robert approached him.

"Mr. Gold, my name is Robert Sandy. I am a surgeon at the Radcliffe. I wonder if you can help me."

"I'll do my best, Mr. Sandy. Please sit down."

"Well, it's an odd story," Robert Sandy said. "I recently operated on one of the Saudi princes. He's in his third year at Magdalen and he'd been involved in a nasty car accident. And now he has given me, or rather his father has given me, a fairly wonderful-looking diamond."

"Good gracious me," Mr. Gold said. "How very exciting."

"I didn't want to accept it, but I'm afraid it was more or less forced on me."

"And you would like me to look at it?"

"Yes, I would. You see, I haven't the faintest idea whether it's worth five hundred pounds or five thousand, and it's only sensible that I should know roughly what the value is."

"Of course you should," Harry Gold said. "I'll be glad to help you. Doctors at the Radcliffe have helped *me* a great deal over the years."

Robert Sandy took the black pouch out of his pocket and placed it on the desk. Harry Gold opened the pouch and tipped the diamond into his hand. As the stone fell into his palm, there was a moment when the old man appeared to freeze. His whole body became motionless as he sat there staring at the brilliant shining thing that lay before him. Slowly, he stood up. He walked over to the window and held the stone so that daylight fell upon it. He turned it over with one finger. He didn't say a word. His expression never changed. Still holding the diamond, he returned to his desk and from a drawer he took out a single sheet of clean white paper. He made a loose fold in the paper and placed the diamond in the fold. Then he returned to the window and stood there for a full minute studying the diamond that lay in the fold of paper.

"I am looking at the color," he said at last. "That's the first thing to do. One always does that against a fold of white paper and preferably in a north light."

"Is that a north light?"

"Yes, it is. This stone is a wonderful color, Mr. Sandy. As fine a D color as I've ever seen. In the trade, the very best quality white is called a D color. In some places it's called a River. That's mostly in Scandinavia. A layman would call it a Blue White."

"It doesn't look very blue to me," Robert Sandy said.

"The purest whites always contain a trace of blue," Harry Gold said. "That's why in the old days they always put a blue-bag into the washing water. It made the clothes whiter."

"Ah yes, of course."

Harry Gold went back to his desk and took out from another drawer a sort of hooded magnifying glass. "This is a ten-times loupe," he said, holding it up.

"What did you call it?"

"A loupe. It is simply a jeweler's magnifier. With this, I can examine the stone for imperfections."

Back once again at the window, Harry Gold began a minute examination of the diamond through the ten-times loupe, holding the paper with the stone on it in one hand and the loupe in the other. This process took maybe four minutes. Robert Sandy watched him and kept quiet.

"So far as I can see," Harry Gold said, "it is completely flawless. It really is a most lovely stone. The quality is superb and the cutting is very fine, though definitely not modern."

"Approximately how many facets would there be on a diamond like that?" Robert Sandy asked.

"Fifty-eight."

"You mean you know exactly?"

"Yes, I know exactly."

"Good Lord. And what roughly would you say it is worth?"

"A diamond like this," Harry Gold said, taking it from the paper and placing it in his palm, "a D color stone of this size and clarity would command on inquiry a trade price of between twenty-five and thirty thousand dollars a carat. In the shops it would cost you double that. Up to sixty thousand dollars a carat in the retail market."

"Great Scott!" Robert Sandy cried, jumping up. The little jeweler's words seemed to have lifted him clean out of his seat. He stood there, stunned.

"And now," Harry Gold was saying, "we must find out precisely how many carats it weighs." He crossed over to a shelf on which there stood a small metal apparatus. "This is simply an electronic scale," he said. He slid back a glass door and placed the diamond inside. He twiddled a couple of knobs, then he read off the figures on a dial. "It weighs fifteen point two seven carats," he said. "And that, in case it interests you, makes it worth about half a million dollars in the trade and over one million dollars if you bought it in a shop."

"You are making me nervous," Robert Sandy said, laughing nervously.

"If I owned it," Harry Gold said, "it would make *me* nervous. Sit down again, Mr. Sandy, so you don't faint."

Robert Sandy sat down.

Harry Gold took his time settling himself into his chair behind the big partner's desk. "This is quite an occasion, Mr. Sandy," he said. "I don't often have the pleasure of giving someone quite such a startlingly wonderful shock as this. I think I'm enjoying it more than you are."

"I am too shocked to be really enjoying it yet," Robert Sandy said. "Give me a moment or two to recover."

"Mind you," Harry Gold said, "one wouldn't expect much less from the king of the Saudis. Did you save the young prince's life?"

"I suppose I did, yes."

"Then that explains it." Harry Gold had put the diamond back on to the fold of white paper on his desk, and he sat there looking at it with the eyes of a man who loved what he saw. "My guess is that this stone came from the treasure chest of old King Ibn Saud of Arabia. If that is the case, then it will be totally unknown in the trade, which makes it even more desirable. Are you going to sell it?"

"Oh gosh, I don't know what I am going to do with it," Robert Sandy said. "It's all so sudden and confusing."

"May I give you some advice?"

"Please do."

"If you *are* going to sell it, you should take it to auction. An unseen stone like this would attract a lot of interest, and the wealthy private buyers would be sure to come in and bid against the trade. And if you were able to reveal its provenance as well, telling them that it came directly from the Saudi Royal Family, then the price would go through the roof."

"You have been more than kind to me," Robert Sandy said. "When I do decide to sell it, I shall come first of all to you for advice. But tell me, does a diamond really cost twice as much in the shops as it does in the trade?"

"I shouldn't be telling you this," Harry Gold said, "but I'm afraid it does."

"So if you buy one in Bond Street or anywhere else like that, you are actually paying twice its intrinsic worth?"

"That's more or less right. A lot of young ladies have received nasty shocks when they've tried to resell jewelry that has been given to them by gentlemen."

"So diamonds are not a girl's best friend?"

"They are still very friendly things to have," Harry Gold said, "as you have just found out. But they are not generally a good investment for the amateur."

Outside in the High, Robert Sandy mounted his bicycle and headed for home. He was feeling totally light-headed. It was as though he had just finished a whole bottle of good wine all by himself. Here he was, solid old Robert Sandy, sedate and sensible, cycling through the streets of Oxford with more than half a million dollars in the pocket of his old tweed jacket! It was madness. But it was true.

He arrived back at his house in Acacia Road at about half past four and parked his bike in the garage alongside the car. Suddenly he found himself running along the little concrete path that led to the front door. "Now stop that!" he said aloud, pulling up short. "Calm down. You've got to make this really good for Betty. Unfold it slowly." But oh, he simply *could not wait* to give the news to his lovely wife and watch her face as he told her the whole story of his afternoon. He found her in the kitchen packing some jars of homemade jam into a basket.

"Robert!" she cried, delighted as always to see him. "You're home early! How nice!"

He kissed her and said, "I *am* a bit early, aren't I?"

"You haven't forgotten we're going to the Renshaws for the weekend? We have to leave fairly soon."

"I had forgotten," he said. "Or maybe I hadn't. Perhaps that's why I'm home early."

"I thought I'd take Margaret some jam."

"Good," he said. "Very good. You take her some jam. That's a very good idea to take Margaret some jam."

There was something in the way he was acting that made her swing round and stare at him. "Robert," she said, "what's happened? There's something the matter."

"Pour us each a drink," he said. "I've got a bit of news for you."

"Oh darling, it's not something awful, is it?"

"No," he said. "It's something funny. I think you'll like it."

"You've been made Head of Surgery!"

"It's funnier than that," he said. "Go on, make a good stiff drink for each of us and sit down and I'll tell you."

"It's a bit early for drinks," she said, but she got the ice tray from the fridge and started making his whiskey and soda. While she was doing this, she kept glancing up at him nervously. She said, "I don't think I've ever seen you quite like this before. You are wildly excited about something and you are pretending to be very calm. You're all red in the face. Are you sure it's good news?"

"I *think* it is," he said, "but I'll let you judge that for yourself." He sat down at the kitchen table and watched her as she put the glass of whiskey in front of him.

"All right," she said. "Come on. Let's have it."

"Get a drink for yourself first," he said.

"My goodness, what is this?" she said, but she poured some gin into a glass and was reaching for the ice tray when he said, "More than that. Give yourself a good stiff one."

"Now I *am* worried," she said, but she did as she was told and then added ice and filled the glass up with tonic. "Now then," she said, sitting down beside him at the table, "get it off your chest."

Robert began telling his story. He started with the prince in the consulting room and he spun it out long and well so that it took a good ten minutes before he came to the diamond.

"It must be quite a whopper," she said, "to make you go all red in the face and funny looking."

He reached into his pocket and took out the little black pouch and put it on the table. "There it is," he said. "What do you think?"

She loosened the silk cord and tipped the stone into her hand. "Oh, my God!" she cried. "It's absolutely stunning!"

"It is, isn't it."

"It's amazing."

"I haven't told you the whole story yet," he said, and while his wife rolled the diamond from the palm of one hand to the other, he went on to tell her about his visit to Harry Gold in the High. When he came to the point where the jeweler began to talk about value, he stopped and said, "So what do you think he said it was worth?"

"Something pretty big," she said. "It's bound to be. I mean just *look* at it!"

"Go on then, make a guess. How much?"

"Ten thousand pounds?" she said. "I really don't have any idea."

"Try again."

"You mean, it's more?"

"Yes, it's quite a lot more."

"Twenty thousand pounds!"

"Would you be thrilled if it was worth as much as that?"

"Of course, I would, darling. Is it really worth twenty thousand pounds?"

"Yes," he said. "And the rest."

"Now don't be a beast, Robert. Just tell me what Mr. Gold said."

"Take another drink of gin."

She did so, then put down the glass, looking at him and waiting.

"It is worth at least half a million dollars and very probably over a million."

"You're joking!" Her words came out in a kind of gasp.

"It's known as a pear shape," he said. "And where it comes to a point at this end, it's as sharp as a needle."

"I'm completely stunned," she said, still gasping.

"You wouldn't have thought half a million, would you?"

"I've never in my life had to think in those sort of figures," she said. She stood up and went over to him and gave him a huge hug and a kiss. "You really are the most wonderful and stupendous man in the world!" she cried.

"I was totally bowled over," he said. "I still am."

"Oh Robert!" she cried, gazing at him with eyes bright as two stars. "Do you realize what this means? It means we can get Diana and her husband out of that horrid little flat and buy them a small house!"

"By golly, you're right!"

"And we can buy a decent flat for John and give him a better allowance all the way through his medical school! And Ben . . . Ben wouldn't have to go on a motorbike to work all through the freezing winters. We could get him something better. And . . . and . . . and . . ."

"And what?" he asked, smiling at her.

"And you and I can take a really good holiday for once and go wherever we please! We can go to Egypt and Turkey and you can visit Baalbek and all the other places you've been longing to go to for years and years!" She was quite breathless with the vista of small pleasures that were unfolding in her dreams. "And you can start collecting some really nice pieces for once in your life as well!"

Ever since he had been a student, Robert Sandy's passion had been the history of the Mediterranean countries, Italy, Greece, Turkey, Syria, and Egypt, and he had made himself into something of an expert on the ancient world of those various civilizations. He had done it by reading and studying and by visiting, when he had the time, the British Museum and the Ashmolean. But with three children to educate and with a job that paid only a reasonable salary, he had never been able to indulge this passion as he would have liked. He wanted above all to visit some of the grand remote regions of Asia Minor and also the now below-ground village of Babylon in Iraq and he would love to see the Arch of Ctsephon and the Sphinx at Memphis and a hundred other things and places, but neither the time nor the money had ever been available. Even so, the long coffee table in the living room was covered with small objects and fragments that he had managed to pick up cheaply here and there through his life. There was a mysterious pale alabaster ushaptiu in the form of a mummy from Upper Egypt which he knew was Pre-Dynastic from about 7000 B.C. There was a bronze bowl from Lydia with an engraving on it of a horse, and an early Byzantine twisted silver necklace, and a section of a wooden painted mask from an Egyptian sarcophagus, and a Roman redware bowl, and a small black Etruscan dish, and perhaps fifty other fragile and interesting little pieces. None was particularly valuable, but Robert Sandy loved them all.

"Wouldn't that be marvelous?" his wife was saying. "Where shall we go first?"

"Turkey," he said.

"Listen," she said, pointing to the diamond that lay sparkling on the kitchen table, "you'd better put your fortune away somewhere safe before you lose it."

"Today is Friday," he said. "When do we get back from the Renshaws?"

"Sunday night."

"And what are we going to do with our million-pound rock in the meanwhile? Take it with us in my pocket?"

"No," she said, "that would be silly. You really cannot walk around with a million pounds in your pocket for a whole weekend. It's got to go into a safe-deposit box at the bank. We should do it now."

"It's Friday night, my darling. All the banks are closed till next Monday."

"So they are," she said. "Well then, we'd better hide it somewhere in the house."

"The house will be empty till we come back," he said. "I don't think that's a very good idea."

"It's better than carrying it around in your pocket or in my handbag."

"I'm not leaving it in the house. An empty house is always liable to be burgled."

"Come on, darling," she said, "surely we can think of a place where no one could possibly find it."

"In the teapot," he said.

"Or bury it in the sugar-basin," she said.

"Or put it in the bowl of one of my pipes in the pipe-rack," he said. "With some tobacco over it."

"Or under the soil of the azalea plant," she said.

"Hey, that's not bad, Betty. That's the best so far."

They sat at the kitchen table with the shining stone lying there between them, wondering very seriously what to do with it for the next two days while they were away.

"I still think it's best if I take it with me," he said.

"I don't, Robert. You'll be feeling in your pocket every five minutes to make sure it's still there. You won't relax for one moment."

"I suppose you're right," he said. "Very well, then. *Shall* we bury it under the soil of the azalea plant in the sitting-room? No one's going to look there."

"It's not one hundred percent safe," she said. "Someone could knock the pot over and the soil would spill out on the floor and presto, there's a sparkling diamond lying there."

"It's a thousand to one against that," he said. "It's a thousand to one against the house being broken into anyway."

"No, it's not," she said. "Houses are being burgled every day. It's not worth chancing it. But look, darling, I'm not going to let this thing become a nuisance to you, or a worry."

"I agree with that," he said.

They sipped their drinks for a while in silence.

"I've got it!" she cried, leaping up from her chair. "I've thought of a marvelous place!"

"Where?"

"In here," she cried, picking up the ice tray and pointing to one of the empty compartments. "We'll just drop it in here and fill it with water and put it back in the fridge. In an hour or two it'll be hidden inside a solid block of ice, and even if you looked, you wouldn't be able to see it."

Robert Sandy stared at the ice tray. "It's fantastic!" he said. "You're a genius! Let's do it right away!"

"Shall we really do it?"

"Of course. It's a terrific idea."

She picked up the diamond and placed it into one of the little empty compartments. She went to the sink and carefully filled the whole tray with water. She opened the door of the freezer section of the fridge and slid the tray in. "It's the top tray on the left," she said. "We'd better remember that. And it'll be in the block of ice furthest away on the righthand side of the tray."

"The top tray on the left," he said. "Got it. I feel better now that it's tucked safely away."

"Finish your drink, darling," she said. "Then we must be off. I've packed your case for you. And we'll try not to think about our million pounds any more until we come back."

"Do we talk about it to other people?" he asked her. "Like the Renshaws or anyone else who might be there?"

"I wouldn't," she said. "It's such an incredible story that it would soon spread around all over the place. Next thing you know, it would be in the papers."

"I don't think the king of the Saudis would like that," he said.

"Nor do I. So let's say nothing at the moment."

"I agree," he said. "I would hate any kind of publicity."

"You'll be able to get yourself a new car," she said, laughing.

"So I will. I'll get one for you, too. What kind would you like, darling?"

"I'll think about it," she said.

Soon after that, the two of them drove off to the Renshaws for the weekend. It wasn't far, just beyond Whitney, some thirty minutes from their own house. Charlie Renshaw was a consultant physician at the hospital and the families had known each other for many years.

The weekend was pleasant and uneventful, and on Sunday evening Robert and Betty Sandy drove home again, arriving at the house in Acacia Road at about seven P.M. Robert took the two small suitcases from the car and they walked up the path together. He unlocked the front door and held it open for his wife.

"I'll make some scrambled eggs," she said, "and crispy bacon. Would you like a drink first, darling?"

"Why not?" he said.

He closed the door and was about to carry the suitcases upstairs when he heard a piercing scream from the sitting room *"Oh no!"* she was crying. *"No! No! No!"*

Robert dropped the suitcase and rushed in after her. She was standing there pressing her hands to her cheeks and already tears were streaming down her face.

The scene in the sitting room was one of utter desolation. The curtains were drawn and they seemed to be the only things that remained intact in the room. Everything else had been smashed to smithereens. All Robert Sandy's precious little objects from the coffee table had been picked up and flung against the walls and were lying in tiny pieces on the carpet. A glass cabinet had been tipped over. A chest of drawers had had its four drawers pulled out and the contents, photograph albums, games of Scrabble and Monopoly, and a chessboard and chessmen and many other family things had been flung across the room. Every single book had been pulled out of the big floor-to-ceiling bookshelves against the far wall and piles of them were now lying open and mutilated all over the place. The glass on each of the four watercolors had been smashed and the oil painting of their three children painted when they were young had had its canvas slashed many times with a knife. The armchairs and the sofa had also been slashed so that the stuffing was bulging out. Virtually everything in the room except the curtains and the carpet had been destroyed.

"Oh, Robert," she said, collapsing into his arms, "I don't think I can stand this."

He didn't say anything. He felt physically sick.

"Stay here," he said. "I'm going to look upstairs." He ran out and took the stairs two at a time and went first to their bedroom. It was the same in there. The drawers had been pulled out and the shirts and blouses and underclothes were now scattered everywhere. The bedclothes had been stripped from the double bed and even the mattress had been tipped off the bed and slashed many times with a knife. The cupboards were open and every dress and suit and every pair of trousers and every jacket and every skirt had been ripped from its hanger. He didn't look in the other bedrooms. He ran downstairs and put an arm around his wife's shoulders and together they picked their way through the debris of the sitting room towards the kitchen. There they stopped.

The mess in the kitchen was indescribable. Almost every single container of any sort in the entire room had been emptied on to the floor and then smashed to pieces. The place was a wasteland of broken jars and bottles and food of every kind. All Betty's homemade jams and pickles and bottled fruits had been swept from the long shelf and lay shattered on the ground. The same had happened to the stuff in the store cupboard, the mayonnaise, the ketchup, the vinegar, the olive oil, the vegetable oil and all the rest. There were two other long shelves on the far wall and on these had stood about twenty lovely large glass jars with big ground-glass stoppers in which were kept rice and flour and brown sugar and bran and oatmeal and all sorts of other things. Every jar now lay on the floor in many pieces, with the contents spewed around. The refrigerator door was open and the things that had been inside, the leftover foods, the milk, the eggs, the butter, the yogurt, the tomatoes, the lettuce, all of them had been pulled out and splashed onto the pretty tiled kitchen floor. The inner drawers of the fridge had been thrown into the mass of slush and trampled on. The plastic ice trays had been yanked out and each had been literally broken in two and thrown aside. Even the plastic-coated shelves had been ripped out of the fridge and bent double and thrown down with the rest. All the bottles of drink, the whiskey, gin, vodka, sherry, vermouth, as well as half a dozen cans of beer, were standing on the table, empty. The bottles of drink and the beer cans seemed to be the only things in the entire house that had not been smashed. Practically the whole floor lay under a thick layer of mush and goo. It was as if a gang of mad children had been told to see how much mess they could make and had succeeded brilliantly.

Robert and Betty Sandy stood on the edge of it all, speechless with horror. At last Robert said, "I imagine our lovely diamond is somewhere underneath all that."

"I don't give a damn about our diamond," Betty said. "I'd like to kill the people who did this."

"So would I," Robert said. "I've got to call the police." He went back into the sitting room and picked up the telephone. By some miracle it still worked.

The first squad car arrived in a few minutes. It was followed over the next half-hour by a police inspector, a couple of plainclothes men, a fingerprint expert, and a photographer.

The inspector had a black moustache and a short muscular body. "These are not professional thieves," he told Robert Sandy after he had taken a look round. "They weren't even amateur thieves. They were simply hooligans off the street. Riff-raff. Yobbos. Probably three of them. People like this scout around looking for an empty house and when they find it they break in and the first thing they do is to hunt out the booze. Did you have much alcohol on the premises?"

"The usual stuff," Robert said. "Whiskey, gin, vodka, sherry, and a few cans of beer."

"They'll have drunk the lot," the inspector said. "Lads like these have only two things in mind, drink and destruction. They collect all the booze on to a table and sit down and drink themselves raving mad. Then they go on the rampage."

"You mean they didn't come in here to steal?" Robert asked.

"I doubt they've stolen anything at all," the inspector said. "If they'd been thieves they would at least have taken your TV set. Instead, they smashed it up."

"But why do they do this?"

"You'd better ask their parents," the inspector said. "They're rubbish, that's all they are, just rubbish. People aren't brought up right any more these days."

Then Robert told the inspector about the diamond. He gave him all the details from the beginning to end because he realized that from the police point of view it was likely to be the most important part of the whole business.

"Half a million quid!" cried the inspector. "Jesus Christ!"

"Probably double that," Robert said.

"Then that's the first thing we look for," the inspector said.

"I personally do not propose to go down on my hands and knees grubbing around in that pile of slush," Robert said. "I don't feel like it at this moment."

"Leave it to us," the inspector said. "We'll find it. That was a clever place to hide it."

"My wife thought of it. But tell me, inspector, if by some remote chance they *had* found it . . ."

"Impossible," the inspector said. "How could they?"

"They might have seen it lying on the floor after the ice had melted," Robert said. "I agree it's unlikely. But if they *had* spotted it, would they have taken it?"

"I think they would," the inspector said. "No one can resist a diamond. It has a sort of magnetism about it. Yes, if one of them had seen it on the floor, I think he would have slipped it into his pocket. But don't worry about it, doctor. It'll turn up."

"I'm not worrying about it," Robert said. "Right now, I'm worrying about my wife and about our house. My wife spent years trying to make this place into a good home."

"Now look, sir," the inspector said, "the thing for you to do tonight is to take your wife off to a hotel and get some rest. Come back tomorrow, both of you, and we'll start sorting things out. There'll be someone here all the time looking after the house."

"I have to operate at the hospital first thing in the morning," Robert said. "But I expect my wife will try to come along."

"Good," the inspector said. "It's a nasty upsetting business having your house ripped apart like this. It's a big shock. I've seen it many times. It hits you very hard."

Robert and Betty Sandy stayed the night at Oxford's Randolph Hotel, and by eight o'clock the following morning Robert was in the operating theater at the hospital, beginning to work his way through his morning list.

Shortly after noon, Robert had finished his last operation, a straightforward nonmalignant prostate on an elderly male. He removed his rubber gloves and mask and went next door to the surgeons' small rest room for a cup of coffee. But before he got his coffee, he picked up the telephone and called his wife.

"How are you, darling?" he said.

"Oh Robert, it's so *awful*," she said. "I just don't know where to begin."

"Have you called the insurance company?"

"Yes, they're coming any moment to help me make a list."

"Good," he said. "And have the police found our diamond?"

"I'm afraid not," she said. "They've been through every bit of that slush in the kitchen and they swear it's not there."

"Then where can it have gone? Do you think the vandals found it?"

"I suppose they must have," she said. "When they broke those ice trays all the ice cubes would have fallen out. They fall out when you just bend the tray. They're meant to."

"They still wouldn't have spotted it in the ice," Robert said.

"They would when the ice melted," she said. "Those men must have been in the house for hours. Plenty of time for it to melt."

"I suppose you're right."

"It would stick out a mile lying there on the floor," she said, "the way it shines."

"Oh dear," Robert said.

"If we never get it back we won't miss it much anyway, darling," she said. "We only had it a few hours."

"I agree," he said. "Do the police have any leads on who the vandals were?"

"Not a clue," she said. "They found lots of fingerprints, but they don't seem to belong to any known criminals."

"They wouldn't," he said, "not if they were hooligans off the street."

"That's what the inspector said."

"Look, darling," he said, "I've just about finished here for the morning. I'm going to grab some coffee, then I'll come home to give you a hand."

"Good," she said. "I need you, Robert. I need you badly."

"Just give me five minutes to rest my feet," he said, "I feel exhausted."

In Number Two Operating Theater not ten yards away, another senior surgeon called Brian Goff was also nearly finished for the morning. He was on his last patient, a young man who had a piece of bone lodged somewhere in his small intestine. Goff was being assisted by a rather jolly young registrar named William Haddock, and between them they had opened the patient's abdomen and Goff was lifting out a section of the small intestine and feeling along it with his fingers. It was routine stuff and there was a good deal of conversation going on in the room.

"Did I ever tell you about the man who had lots of little live fish in his bladder?" William Haddock was saying.

"I don't think you did," Goff said.

"When we were students at Barts," William Haddock said, "we were being taught by a particularly unpleasant professor of Urology. One day, this twit was going to demonstrate how to examine the bladder using a cystoscope. The patient was an old man suspected of having stones. Well now, in one of the hospital waiting rooms, there was an aquarium that was full of those tiny little fish, neons they're called, brilliant colors, and one of the students sucked up about twenty of them into a syringe and managed to inject them into the patient's bladder when he was under his pre-med, before he was taken up to theater for his cystoscopy."

"That's disgusting!" the theater sister cried. "You can stop right there, Mr. Haddock!"

Brian Goff smiled behind his mask and said, "What happened next?" As he spoke, he had about three feet of the patient's small intestine lying on the green sterile sheet, and he was still feeling along it with his fingers.

"When the professor got the cystoscope into the bladder and put his eye to it," William Haddock said, "he started jumping up and down and shouting with excitement.

"'What is it, sir?' the guilty student asked him. 'What do you see?'"

"'It's fish!' cried the professor. 'There's hundreds of little fish! They're swimming about!'"

"You made it up," the theater sister said. "It's not true."

"It most certainly is true," the registrar said. "I looked down the cystoscope myself and saw the fish. And they were actually swimming about."

"We might have expected a fishy story from a man with a name like Haddock," Goff said. "Here we are," he added. "Here's this poor chap's trouble. You want to feel it?"

William Haddock took the pale gray piece of intestine between his fingers and pressed. "Yes," he said. "Got it."

"And if you look just there," Goff said, instructing him, "you can see where the bit of bone has punctured the mucosa. It's already inflamed."

Brian Goff held the section of intestine in the palm of his left hand. The sister handed him a scalpel and he made a small incision. The sister gave him a pair of forceps and Goff probed down amongst all the slushy matter of the intestine until he found the offending object. He brought it out, held firmly in the forceps, and dropped it into the small stainless-steel bowl the sister was holding. The thing was covered in pale brown gunge.

"That's it," Goff said. "You can finish this one for me now, can't you, William. I was meant to be at a meeting downstairs fifteen minutes ago."

"You go ahead," William Haddock said. "I'll close him up."

The senior surgeon hurried out of the theater and the registrar proceeded to sew up, first the incision in the intestine, then the abdomen itself. The whole thing took no more than a few minutes.

"I'm finished," he said to the anesthetist.

The man nodded and removed the mask from the patient's face.

"Thank you, sister," William Haddock said. "See you tomorrow." As he moved away, he picked up from the sister's tray the stainless-steel bowl that contained the gunge-covered brown object. "Ten to one it's a chicken bone," he said and he carried it to the sink and began rinsing it under the tap.

"Good God, what's this?" he cried. "Come and look, sister!"

The sister came over to look. "It's a piece of costume jewelry," she said. "Probably part of a necklace. Now how on earth did he come to swallow that?"

"He'd have passed it if it hadn't had such a sharp point," William Haddock said. "I think I'll give it to my girlfriend."

"You can't do that, Mr. Haddock," the sister said. "It belongs to the patient. Hang on a sec. Let me look at it again." She took the stone from William Haddock's gloved hand and carried it into the powerful

light that hung over the operating table. The patient had now been lifted off the table and was being wheeled out into Recovery next door, accompanied by the anesthetist.

"Come here, Mr. Haddock," the sister said, and there was an edge of excitement in her voice. William Haddock joined her under the light. "This is amazing," she went on. "Just look at the way it sparkles and shines. A bit of glass wouldn't do that."

"Maybe it's rock crystal," William Haddock said, "or topaz, one of those semi-precious stones."

"You know what I think," the sister said. "I think it's a diamond."

"Don't be damn silly," William Haddock said.

A junior nurse was wheeling away the instrument trolley and a male theater assistant was helping to clear up. Neither of them took any notice of the young surgeon and the sister. The sister was about twenty-eight years old, and now that she had removed her mask she appeared as an extremely attractive young lady.

"It's easy enough to test it," William Haddock said. "See if it cuts glass."

Together they crossed over to the frosted-glass window of the operating room. The sister held the stone between finger and thumb and pressed the sharp pointed end against the glass and drew it downward. There was a fierce scraping crunch as the point bit into the glass and left a deep line two inches long.

"Jesus Christ!" William Haddock said. "It *is* a diamond!"

"If it is, it belongs to the patient," the sister said firmly.

"Maybe it does," William Haddock said, "but he was mighty glad to get rid of it. Hold on a moment. Where are his notes?" He hurried over to the side table and picked up a folder which said on it JOHN

DIGGS. He opened the folder. In it there was an X ray of the patient's intestine accompanied by the radiologist's report. *John Diggs,* the report said. *Age 17. Address 123 Mayfield Road, Oxford. There is clearly a large obstruction of some sort in the upper small intestine. The patient has no rec-ollection of swallowing anything unusual, but says that he ate some fried chicken on Sunday evening. The object clearly has a sharp point that has pierced the mucosa of the intestine, and it could be a piece of bone . . .*

"How could he swallow a thing like that without knowing it?" William Haddock said.

"It doesn't make sense," the sister said.

"There's no question it's a diamond after the way it cut the glass," William Haddock said. "Do you agree?"

"Absolutely," the sister said.

"And a bloody big one at that," Haddock said. "The question is, how good a diamond is it? How much is it worth?"

"We'd better send it to the lab right away," the sister said.

"To hell with the lab," Haddock said. "Let's have a bit of fun and do it ourselves."

"How?"

"We'll take it to Gold's, the jeweler's in the High. They'll know. The damn thing must be worth a fortune. We're not going to steal it, but we're damn well going to find out about it. Are you game?"

"Do you know anyone at Gold's?" the sister said.

"No, but that doesn't matter. Do you have a car?"

"My Mini's in the car park."

"Right. Get changed. I'll meet you out there. It's about your lunch time anyway. I'll take the stone."

Twenty minutes later, at a quarter to one, the little Mini pulled up outside the jewelry shop of H. F. Gold and parked on the double yellow lines. "Who cares," William Haddock said. "We won't be long." He and the sister went into the shop.

There were two customers inside, a young man and a girl. They were examining a tray of rings and were being served by the woman assistant. As soon as they came in, the assistant pressed a bell under the counter and Harry Gold emerged through the door at the back. "Yes," he said to William Haddock and the sister. "Can I help you?"

"Would you mind telling us what this is worth?" William Haddock said, placing the stone on a piece of green cloth that lay on the counter.

Harry Gold stopped dead. He stared at the stone. Then he looked up at the young man and woman who stood before him. He was thinking very fast. Steady now, he told himself. Don't do anything silly. Act natural.

"Well, well," he said as casually as he could. "That looks to me like a very fine diamond, a very fine diamond indeed. Would you mind waiting a moment while I weigh it and examine it carefully in my office? Then perhaps I'll be able to give you an accurate valuation. Do sit down, both of you."

Harry Gold scuttled back into his office with the diamond in his hand. Immediately, he took it to the electronic scale and weighed it. Fifteen point two seven carats. That was exactly the weight of Mr. Robert Sandy's stone! He had been certain it was the same one the moment he saw it. Who could mistake a diamond like that? And now the weight had proved it. His instinct was to call the police right away, but he was a cautious man who did not like making mistakes. Perhaps the doctor had already sold his diamond. Perhaps he had given it to his children. Who knows?

Quickly he picked up the Oxford telephone book. The Radcliffe Infirmary was Oxford 249891. He dialled it. He asked for Mr. Robert Sandy. He got Robert's secretary. He told her it was most urgent that he speak to Mr. Sandy this instant. The secretary said, "Hold on, please." She called the operating theater. Mr. Sandy had gone home half an hour ago, they told her. She took up the outside phone and relayed this information to Mr. Gold.

"What's his home number?" Mr. Gold asked her.

"Is this to do with a patient?"

"No!" cried Harry Gold. "It's to do with a robbery! For heaven's sake, woman, give me that number quickly!"

"Who is speaking, please?"

"Harry Gold! I'm the jeweler in the High! Don't waste time, I beg you!"

She gave him the number.

Harry Gold dialed again.

"Mr. Sandy?"

"Speaking."

"This is Harry Gold, Mr. Sandy, the jeweler. Have you by any chance lost your diamond?"

"Yes, I have."

"Two people have just brought it into my shop," Harry Gold whispered excitedly. "A man and a woman. Youngish. They're trying to get it valued. They're waiting out there now."

"Are you certain it's my stone?"

"Positive. I weighed it."

"Keep them there, Mr. Gold!" Robert Sandy cried. "Talk to them! Humor them! Do anything! I'm calling the police!"

Robert Sandy called the police station. Within seconds, he was giving the news to the detective inspector who was in charge of the case. "Get there fast and you'll catch them both!" he said. "I'm on my way, too!"

"Come on, darling!" he shouted to his wife. "Jump in the car. I think they've found our diamond and the thieves are in Harry Gold's shop right now trying to sell it!"

When Robert and Betty Sandy drove up to Harry Gold's shop nine minutes later, two police cars were already parked outside. "Come on, darling," Robert said. "Let's go in and see what's happening."

There was a good deal of activity inside the shop when Robert and Betty Sandy rushed in. Two policemen and two plainclothes detectives, one of them the inspector, were surrounding a furious William Haddock and an even more furious theater sister. Both the young surgeon and the theater sister were handcuffed.

"You found it *where?*" the inspector was saying.

"Take these damn handcuffs off me!" the sister was shouting. "How dare you do this!"

"Tell us again where you found it," the inspector said, caustic.

"In someone's stomach!" William Haddock yelled back at him. "I've told you twice!"

"Don't give me that crap!" the inspector said.

"Good God, William!" Robert Sandy cried as he came in and saw who it was. "And Sister Wyman! What on earth are you two doing here?"

"They had the diamond," the inspector said. "They were trying to flog it. Do you know these people, Mr. Sandy?"

It didn't take very long for William Haddock to explain to Robert

Sandy, and indeed to the inspector, exactly how and where the diamond had been found.

"Remove their handcuffs, for heaven's sake, inspector," Robert Sandy said. "They're telling the truth. The man you want, at least one of the men you want, is in the hospital right now, just coming round from his anesthetic. Isn't that right, William?"

"Correct," William Haddock said. "His name is John Diggs. He'll be in one of the surgical wards."

Harry Gold stepped forward. "Here's your diamond, Mr. Sandy," he said.

"Now listen," the theater sister said, still angry, "would someone for God's sake tell me how that patient came to swallow a diamond like this without knowing he'd done it?"

"I think I can guess," Robert Sandy said. "He allowed himself the luxury of putting ice in his drink. Then he got very drunk. Then he swallowed a piece of half-melted ice."

"I still don't get it," the sister said.

"I'll tell you the rest later," Robert Sandy said. "In fact, why don't we all go round the corner and have a drink ourselves."

Dip in the Pool

On the morning of the third day, the sea calmed. Even the most delicate passengers—those who had not been seen around the ship since sailing time—emerged from their cabins and crept on to the sundeck where the deck steward gave them chairs and tucked rugs around their legs and left them lying in rows, their faces upturned to the pale, almost heatless January sun.

It had been moderately rough the first two days, and this sudden calm and the sense of comfort that it brought created a more genial atmosphere over the whole ship. By the time evening came, the passengers, with twelve hours of good weather behind them, were beginning to feel confident, and at eight o'clock that night the main dining room was filled with people eating and drinking with the assured, complacent air of seasoned sailors.

The meal was not half over when the passengers became aware, by the slight friction between their bodies and the seats of their chairs, that the big ship had actually started rolling again. It was very gentle at first, just a slow, lazy leaning to one side, then to the other, but it was enough to cause a subtle, immediate change of mood over the whole room. A few of the passengers glanced up from their food, hesitating, waiting, almost listening for the next roll, smiling nervously, little secret glimmers of apprehension in their eyes. Some were completely unruffled, some were openly smug, a number of the smug ones making jokes about food and weather in order to torture the few who were beginning to suffer. The movement of the ship then became rapidly more and more violent, and only five or six minutes after the first roll had been noticed, she was swinging heavily from side to side, the passengers bracing themselves in their chairs, leaning against the pull as in a car cornering.

At last the really bad roll came, and Mr. William Botibol, sitting at the purser's table, saw his plate of poached turbot with hollandaise sauce sliding suddenly away from under his fork. There was a flutter of excitement, everybody reaching for plates and wineglasses. Mrs. Renshaw, seated at the purser's right, gave a little scream and clutched that gentleman's arm.

"Going to be a dirty night," the purser said, looking at Mrs. Renshaw. "I think it's blowing up for a very dirty night."

There was just the faintest suggestion of relish in the way the purser said this.

A steward came hurrying up and sprinkled water on the tablecloth between the plates. The excitement subsided. Most of the passengers continued with their meal. A small number, including Mrs. Renshaw, got carefully to their feet and threaded their way with a kind of concealed haste between the tables and through the doorway.

"Well," the purser said, "there she goes." He glanced around with approval at the remainder of his flock, who were sitting quiet, looking complacent, their faces reflecting openly that extraordinary pride that travelers seem to take in being recognized as "good sailors."

When the eating was finished and the coffee had been served, Mr. Botibol, who had been unusually grave and thoughtful since the rolling started, suddenly stood up and carried his cup of coffee around to Mrs. Renshaw's vacant place, next to the purser. He seated himself in the chair, then immediately leaned over and began to whisper urgently in the purser's ear. "Excuse me," he said, "but could you tell me something, please?"

The purser, small and fat and red, bent forward to listen. "What's the trouble, Mr. Botibol?"

"What I want to know is this." The man's face was anxious and the purser was watching it. "What I want to know is will the captain already have made his estimate on the day's run—you know, for the auction pool? I mean before it began to get rough like this?"

The purser, who had prepared himself to receive a personal confidence, smiled and leaned back in his seat to relax his full belly. "I should say so—yes," he answered. He didn't bother to whisper his reply, although automatically he lowered his voice, as one does when answering a whisperer.

"About how long ago do you think he did it?"

"Some time this afternoon. He usually does it in the afternoon."

"About what time?"

"Oh, I don't know. Around four o'clock I should guess."

"Now tell me another thing. How does the captain decide which number it shall be? Does he take a lot of trouble over that?"

The purser looked at the anxious frowning face of Mr. Botibol and he smiled, knowing quite well what the man was driving at. "Well, you see, the captain has a little conference with the navigating officer, and they study the weather and a lot of other things, and then they make their estimate."

Mr. Botibol nodded, pondering this answer for a moment. Then he said, "Do you think the captain knew there was bad weather coming today?"

"I couldn't tell you," the purser replied. He was looking into the small black eyes of the other man, seeing the two single little specks of excitement dancing in their centers. "I really couldn't tell you, Mr. Botibol. I wouldn't know."

"If this gets any worse it might be worth buying some of the low numbers. What do you think?" The whispering was more urgent, more anxious now.

"Perhaps it will," the purser said. "I doubt whether the old man allowed for a really rough night. It was pretty calm this afternoon when he made his estimate."

The others at the table had become silent and were trying to hear, watching the purser with that intent, half-cocked, listening look that you can see also at the racetrack when they are trying to overhear a trainer talking about his chance: the slightly open lips, the upstretched eyebrows, the head forward and cocked a little to one side—that desperately straining, half-hypnotized, listening look that comes to all of them when they are hearing something straight from the horse's mouth.

"Now suppose *you* were allowed to buy a number, which one would *you* choose today?" Mr. Botibol whispered.

"I don't know what the range is yet," the purser patiently answered.

"They don't announce the range till the auction starts after dinner. And I'm really not very good at it anyway. I'm only the purser, you know."

At that point Mr. Botibol stood up. "Excuse me, all," he said, and he walked carefully away over the swaying floor between the other tables, and twice he had to catch hold of the back of a chair to steady himself against the ship's roll.

"The sundeck, please," he said to the elevator man.

The wind caught him full in the face as he stepped out on to the open deck. He staggered and grabbed hold of the rail and held on tight with both hands, and he stood there looking out over the darkening sea where the great waves were welling up high and white horses were riding against the wind with plumes of spray behind them as they went.

"Pretty bad out there, wasn't it, sir?" the elevator man said on the way down.

Mr. Botibol was combing his hair back into place with a small red comb. "Do you think we've slackened speed at all on account of the weather?" he asked.

"Oh, my word, yes, sir. We slackened off considerable since this started. You got to slacken off speed in weather like this or you'll be throwing the passengers all over the ship."

Down in the smoking room people were already gathering for the auction. They were grouping themselves politely around the various tables, the men a little stiff in their dinner jackets, a little pink and over-shaved and stiff beside their cool white-armed women. Mr. Botibol took a chair close to the auctioneer's table. He crossed his legs, folded his arms, and settled himself in his seat with the rather desperate air of a man who has made a tremendous decision and refuses to be frightened.

The pool, he was telling himself, would probably be around seven thousand dollars. That was almost exactly what it had been the last two days with the numbers selling for between three and four hundred apiece. Being a British ship they did it in pounds, but he liked to do his thinking in his own currency. Seven thousand dollars was plenty of money. My goodness, yes! And what he would do, he would get them to pay him in hundred-dollar bills and he would take it ashore in the inside pocket of his jacket. No problem there. And right away, yes right away, he would buy a Lincoln convertible. He would pick it up on the way from the ship and drive it home just for the pleasure of seeing Ethel's face when she came out the front door and looked at it. Wouldn't that be something, to see Ethel's face when he glided up to the door in a brand-new pale-green Lincoln convertible! Hullo, Ethel, honey, he would say, speaking very casual. I just thought I'd get you a little present. I saw it in the window as I went by, so I thought of you and how you were always wanting one. You like it, honey? he would say. You like the color? And then he would watch her face.

The auctioneer was standing up behind his table now. "Ladies and gentlemen!" he shouted. "The captain has estimated the day's run ending midday tomorrow, at five hundred and fifteen miles. As usual we will take the ten numbers on either side of it to make up the range. That makes it five hundred and five to five hundred and twenty-five. And of course for those who think the true figure will be still farther away, there'll be 'low field' and 'high field' sold separately as well. Now, we'll draw the first numbers out of the hat . . . here we are . . . five hundred and twelve?"

The room became quiet. The people sat still in their chairs, all eyes watching the auctioneer. There was a certain tension in the air, and as the bids got higher, the tension grew. This wasn't a game or a joke; you could be sure of that by the way one man would look across at another who had raised his bid—smiling perhaps, but only the lips smiling, the eyes bright and absolutely cold.

Number five hundred and twelve was knocked down for one hundred and ten pounds. The next three or four numbers fetched roughly the same amount.

The ship was rolling heavily, and each time she went over, the wooden paneling on the walls creaked as if it were going to split. The passengers held on to the arms of their chairs, concentrating upon the auction.

"Low field!" the auctioneer called out. "The next number is low field."

Mr. Botibol sat up very straight and tense. He would wait, he had decided, until the others had finished bidding, then he would jump in and make the last bid. He had figured that there must be at least five hundred dollars in his account at the bank at home, probably nearer six. That was about two hundred pounds—over two hundred. This ticket wouldn't fetch more than that.

"As you all know," the auctioneer was saying, "low field covers every number *below* the smallest number in the range, in this case every number below five hundred and five. So, if you think this ship is going to cover less than five hundred and five miles in the twenty-four hours ending at noon tomorrow, you better get in and buy this number. So what am I bid?"

It went clear up to one hundred and thirty pounds. Others beside

Mr. Botibol seemed to have noticed that the weather was rough. One hundred and forty . . . fifty . . . There it stopped. The auctioneer raised his hammer.

"Going at one hundred and fifty . . ."

"Sixty!" Mr. Botibol called, and every face in the room turned and looked at him.

"Seventy!"

"Eighty!" Mr. Botibol called.

"Ninety!"

"Two hundred!" Mr. Botibol called. He wasn't stopping now—not for anyone.

There was a pause.

"Any advance on two hundred pounds?"

Sit still, he told himself. Sit absolutely still and don't look up. It's unlucky to look up. Hold your breath. No one's going to bid you up so long as you hold your breath.

"Going for two hundred pounds . . ." The auctioneer had a pink bald head and there were little beads of sweat sparkling on top of it. "Going . . ." Mr. Botibol held his breath. "Going . . . Gone!" The man banged the hammer on the table. Mr. Botibol wrote out a check and handed it to the auctioneer's assistant, then he settled back in his chair to wait for the finish. He did not want to go to bed before he knew how much there was in the pool.

They added it up after the last number had been sold and it came to twenty-one-hundred-odd pounds. That was around six thousand dollars. Ninety percent to go to the winner, ten percent to seamen's charities. Ninety percent of six thousand was five thousand four hundred. Well—that was enough. He could buy the Lincoln convertible and there would be something left over, too. With this gratifying thought he went off, happy and excited, to his cabin.

When Mr. Botibol awoke the next morning he lay quite still for several minutes with his eyes shut, listening for the sound of the gale, waiting for the roll of the ship. There was no sound of any gale and the ship was not rolling. He jumped up and peered out of the porthole. The sea—Oh Jesus God—as smooth as glass, the great ship was moving through it fast, obviously making up for time lost during the night. Mr. Botibol turned away and sat slowly down on the edge of his bunk. A fine electricity of fear was beginning to prickle under the skin of his stomach. He hadn't a hope now. One of the higher numbers was certain to win it after this.

"Oh my God," he said aloud. "What shall I do?"

What, for example, would Ethel say? It was simply not possible to tell her he had spent almost all of their two years' savings on a ticket in the ship's pool. Nor was it possible to keep the matter secret. To do that he would have to tell her to stop drawing checks. And what about the monthly instalments on the television set and the *Encyclopaedia Britannica*? Already he could see the anger and contempt in the woman's eyes, the blue becoming gray and the eyes themselves narrowing as they always did when there was anger in them.

"Oh, my God. What *shall* I do?"

There was no point in pretending that he had the slightest chance now—not unless the goddam ship started to go backwards. They'd have to put her in reverse and go full speed astern and keep right on going if he was to have any chance of winning it now. Well, maybe he should ask the captain to do just that. Offer him ten percent of the profits. Offer him more if he wanted it. Mr. Botibol started to giggle.

Then very suddenly he stopped, his eyes and mouth both opening wide in a kind of shocked surprise. For it was at this moment that the idea came. It hit him hard and quick, and he jumped up from the bed, terribly excited, ran over to the porthole and looked out again. Well, he thought, why not? Why ever not? The sea was calm and he wouldn't have any trouble keeping afloat until they picked him up. He had a vague feeling that someone had done this thing before, but that didn't prevent him from doing it again. The ship would have to stop and lower a boat, and the boat would have to go back maybe half a mile to get him, and then it would have to return to the ship, the whole thing. An hour was about thirty miles. It would knock thirty miles off the day's run. That would do it. "Low field" would be sure to win it then. Just so long as he made certain someone saw him falling over; but that would be simple to arrange. And he'd better wear light clothes, something easy to swim in. Sports clothes, that was it. He would dress as though he were going up to play some deck tennis—just a shirt and a pair of shorts and tennis shoes. And leave his watch behind. What was the time? Nine-fifteen. The sooner the better, then. Do it now and get it over with. Have to do it soon, because the time limit was midday.

Mr. Botibol was both frightened and excited when he stepped out on to the sun deck in his sports clothes. His small body was wide at the hips, tapering upward to extremely narrow sloping shoulders, so that it resembled, in shape at any rate, a bollard. His white skinny legs were covered with black hairs, and he came cautiously out on deck, treading softly in his tennis shoes. Nervously he looked around him. There was only one other person in sight, an elderly woman with very thick ankles and immense buttocks who was leaning over the rail staring at the sea. She was wearing a coat of Persian lamb and the collar was turned up so Mr. Botibol couldn't see her face.

He stood still, examining her carefully from a distance. Yes, he told himself, she would probably do. She would probably give the alarm just as quickly as anyone else. But wait one minute, take your time, William Botibol, take your time. Remember what you told yourself a few minutes ago in the cabin when you were changing? You remember that?

The thought of leaping off a ship into the ocean a thousand miles from the nearest land had made Mr. Botibol—a cautious man at the best of times—unusually advertent. He was by no means satisfied yet that this woman he saw before him was *absolutely certain* to give the alarm when he made his jump. In his opinion there were two possible reasons why she might fail him. Firstly, she might be deaf and blind. It was not very probable, but on the other hand it *might* be so, and why take a chance? All he had to do was check it by talking to her for a moment beforehand. Secondly—and this will demonstrate how suspicious the mind of a man can become when it is working through self-preservation and fear—secondly, it had occurred to him that the woman might herself be the owner of one of the high numbers in the pool and as such would have a sound financial reason for not wishing to stop the ship. Mr. Botibol recalled that people had killed their fellows for far less than six thousand dollars. It was happening every day in the newspapers. So why take a chance on that either? Check on it first. Be sure of your facts. Find out about it by a little polite conversation. Then, provided that the woman appeared also to be a pleasant, kindly human being, the thing was a cinch and he could leap overboard with a light heart.

Mr. Botibol advanced casually towards the woman and took up a position beside her, leaning on the rail. "Hullo," he said pleasantly.

She turned and smiled at him, a surprisingly lovely, almost a beautiful smile, although the face itself was very plain. "Hullo," she answered him.

Check, Mr. Botibol told himself, on the first question. She is neither blind nor deaf. "Tell me," he said, coming straight to the point, "what did you think of the auction last night?"

"Auction?" she said, frowning. "Auction? What auction?"

"You know, that silly old thing they have in the lounge after dinner, selling numbers on the ship's daily run. I just wondered what you thought about it."

She shook her head, and again she smiled, a sweet and pleasant smile that had in it perhaps the trace of an apology. "I'm very lazy," she said. "I always go to bed early. I have my dinner in bed. It's so restful to have dinner in bed."

Mr. Botibol smiled back at her and began to edge away. "Got to go and get my exercise now," he said. "Never miss my exercise in the morning. It was nice seeing you. Very nice seeing you . . ." He retreated about ten paces, and the woman let him go without looking around.

Everything was now in order. The sea was calm, he was lightly dressed for swimming, there were almost certainly no man-eating sharks in this part of the Atlantic, and there was this pleasant kindly old woman to give the alarm. It was a question now only of whether the ship would be delayed long enough to swing the balance in his favor. Almost certainly it would. In any event, he could do a little to help in that direction himself. He could make a few difficulties about getting hauled up into the lifeboat. Swim around a bit, back away from them surreptitiously as they tried to come up close to fish him out. Every minute, every second gained would help him win. He began to move forward again to the rail, but now a new fear assailed him. Would he get caught in the propeller? He had heard about that happening to persons falling off the sides of big ships. But then, he wasn't going to fall, he was going to jump, and that was a very different thing. Provided he jumped out far enough he would be sure to clear the propeller.

Mr. Botibol advanced slowly to a position at the rail about twenty yards away from the woman. She wasn't looking at him now. So much the better. He didn't want her watching him as he jumped off. So long as no one was watching he would be able to say afterwards that he had slipped and fallen by accident. He peered over the side of the ship. It was a long, long drop. Come to think of it now, he might easily hurt himself badly if he hit the water flat. Wasn't there someone who once split his stomach open that way, doing a belly flop from the high dive? He must jump straight and land feet first. Go in like a knife. Yes, sir. The water seemed cold and deep and gray and it made him shiver to look at it. But it was now or never. Be a man, William Botibol, be a man. All right then . . . now . . . here goes . . .

He climbed up on to the wide wooden top rail, stood there poised, balancing for three terrifying seconds, then he leaped—he leaped up and out as far as he could go and at the same time he shouted *"Help!"*

"Help! Help!" he shouted as he fell. Then he hit the water and went under.

When the first shout for help sounded, the woman who was leaning on the rail started up and gave a little jump of surprise. She looked around quickly and saw sailing past her through the air this small man dressed in white shorts and tennis shoes, spread-eagled and shouting as he went. For a moment she looked as though she weren't quite sure what she ought to do: throw a lifebelt, run away and give the alarm, or simply turn and yell. She drew back a pace from the rail and swung half around facing up to the bridge, and for this brief moment she remained motionless, tense, undecided. Then almost at once she seemed to relax, and she leaned forward far over the rail, staring at the water where it was turbulent in the ship's wake. Soon a tiny round black head appeared in the foam, an arm raised above it, once, twice, vigorously waving, and a small faraway voice was heard calling something that was difficult to understand. The woman leaned still farther over the rail, trying to keep the little bobbing black speck in sight, but soon, so very soon, it was such a long way away that she couldn't even be sure it was there at all.

After a while another woman came out on deck. This one was bony and angular, and she wore horn-rimmed spectacles. She spotted the first woman and walked over to her, treading the deck in the deliberate, military fashion of all spinsters.

"So *there* you are," she said.

The woman with the fat ankles turned and looked at her, but said nothing.

"I've been searching for you," the bony one continued. "Searching all over."

"It's very odd," the woman with the fat ankles said. "A man dived overboard just now, with his clothes on."

"Nonsense!"

"Oh yes. He said he wanted to get some exercise and he dived in and didn't even bother to take his clothes off."

"You better come down now," the bony woman said. Her mouth

had suddenly become firm, her whole face sharp and alert, and she spoke less kindly than before. "And don't you ever go wandering about on deck alone like this again. You know quite well you're meant to wait for me."

"Yes, Maggie," the woman with the fat ankles answered, and again she smiled, a tender, trusting smile, and she took the hand of the other one and allowed herself to be led away across the deck.

"Such a nice man," she said. "He waved to me."

THE CHAMPION OF THE WORLD

All day, in between serving customers, we had been crouching over the table in the office of the filling station, preparing the raisins. They were plump and soft and swollen from being soaked in water, and when you nicked them with a razor blade the skin sprang open and the jelly stuff inside squeezed out as easily as you could wish.

But we had a hundred and ninety-six of them to do altogether and the evening was nearly upon us before we had finished.

"Don't they look marvelous!" Claud cried, rubbing his hands together hard. "What time is it, Gordon?"

"Just after five."

Through the window we could see a station wagon pulling up at the pumps with a woman at the wheel and about eight children in the back eating ice cream.

"We ought to be moving soon," Claud said. "The whole thing'll be a washout if we don't arrive before sunset, you realize that." He was getting twitchy now. His face had the same flushed and pop-eyed look it got before a dog race or when there was a date with Clarice in the evening.

We both went outside and Claud gave the woman the number of

gallons she wanted. When she had gone, he remained standing in the middle of the driveway squinting anxiously up at the sun which was now only the width of a man's hand above the line of trees along the crest of the ridge on the far side of the valley.

"All right," I said. "Lock up."

He went quickly from pump to pump, securing each nozzle in its holder with a small padlock.

"You'd better take off that yellow pullover," he said.

"Why should I?"

"You'll be shining like a bloody beacon out there in the moonlight."

"I'll be all right."

"You will not," he said. "Take if off, Gordon, please. I'll see you in three minutes." He disappeared into his caravan behind the filling station, and I went indoors and changed my yellow pullover for a blue one.

When we met again outside, Claud was dressed in a pair of black trousers and a dark-green turtleneck sweater. On his head he wore a brown cloth cap with the peak pulled down low over his eyes, and he looked like an apache actor out of a nightclub.

"What's under there?" I asked, seeing the bulge at his waistline.

He pulled up his sweater and showed me two thin but very large white cotton sacks which were bound neat and tight around his belly. "To carry the stuff," he said darkly.

"I see."

"Let's go," he said.

"I still think we ought to take the car."

"It's too risky. They'll see it parked."

"But it's over three miles up to that wood."

"Yes," he said. "And I suppose you realize we can get six months in the clink if they catch us."

"You never told me that."

"Didn't I?"

"I'm not coming," I said. "It's not worth it."

"The walk will do you good, Gordon. Come on."

It was a calm sunny evening with little wisps of brilliant white cloud hanging motionless in the sky, and the valley was cool and very quiet as the two of us began walking together along the grass verge on the side of the road that ran between the hills towards Oxford.

"You got the raisins?" Claud asked.

"They're in my pocket."

"Good," he said. "Marvelous."

Ten minutes later we turned left off the main road into a narrow lane with high hedges on either side and from now on it was all uphill.

"How many keepers are there?" I asked.

"Three."

Claud threw away a half-finished cigarette. A minute later he lit another.

"I don't usually approve of new methods," he said. "Not on this sort of a job."

"Of course."

"But by God, Gordon, I think we're on to a hot one this time."

"You do?"

"There's no question about it."

"I hope you're right."

"It'll be a milestone in the history of poaching," he said. "But don't you go telling a single soul how we've done it, you understand. Because if this ever leaked out we'd have every bloody fool in the district doing the same thing and there wouldn't be a pheasant left."

"I won't say a word."

"You ought to be very proud of yourself," he went on. "There's been men with brains studying this problem for hundreds of years and not one of them's ever come up with anything even a quarter as artful as you have. Why didn't you tell me about it before?"

"You never invited my opinion," I said.

And that was the truth. In fact, up until the day before, Claud had never even offered to discuss with me the sacred subject of poaching. Often enough, on a summer's evening when work was finished, I had seen him with cap on head sliding quietly out of his caravan and dis-appearing up the road towards the woods; and sometimes, watching him through the windows of the filling station, I would find myself wondering exactly what he was going to do, what wily tricks he was go-ing to practice all alone up there under the trees in the dead of night. He seldom came back until very late, and never, absolutely never did he bring any of the spoils with him personally on his return. But the fol-lowing afternoon—and I couldn't imagine how he did it—there would always be a pheasant or a hare or a brace of partridges hanging up in the shed behind the filling station for us to eat.

This summer he had been particularly active, and during the last couple of months he had stepped up the tempo to a point where he was going out four and sometimes five nights a week. But that was not all. It seemed to me that recently his whole attitude towards poaching had undergone a subtle and mysterious change. He was more purposeful about it now, more tight-lipped and intense than before, and I had the impression that this was not so much a game any longer as a crusade, a sort of private war that Claud was waging single-handed against an invisible and hated enemy.

But who?

I wasn't sure about this, but I had a suspicion that it was none other than the famous Mr. Victor Hazel himself, the owner of the land and the pheasants. Mr. Hazel was a local brewer with an unbelievably arrogant manner. He was rich beyond words, and his property stretched for miles along either side of the valley. He was a self-made man with no charm at all and precious few virtues. He loathed all persons of humble station, having once been one of them himself, and he strove desperately to mingle with what he believed were the right kind of folk. He rode to hounds and gave shooting parties and wore fancy waistcoats and every weekday he drove an enormous black Rolls-Royce past the filling station on his way to the brewery. As he flashed by, we would sometimes catch a glimpse of the great glistening brewer's face above the wheel, pink as a ham, all soft and inflamed from drinking too much beer.

Anyway, yesterday afternoon, right out of the blue, Claud had suddenly said to me, "I'll be going on up to Hazel's woods again tonight. Why don't you come along?"

"Who, me?"

"It's about the last chance this year for pheasants," he had said. "The shooting season opens Saturday and the birds'll be scattered all over the place after that—if there's any left."

"Why the sudden invitation?" I had asked, greatly suspicious.

"No special reason, Gordon. No reason at all."

"Is it risky?"

He hadn't answered this.

"I suppose you keep a gun or something hidden away up there?"

"A gun!" he cried, disgusted. "Nobody ever *shoots* pheasants, didn't you know that? You've only got to fire a *cap pistol* in Hazel's woods and the keepers'll be on you."

"Then how do you do it?"

"Ah," he said, and the eyelids drooped over the eyes, veiled and secretive.

There was a long pause. Then he said, "Do you think you could keep your mouth shut if I was to tell you a thing or two?"

"Definitely."

"I've never told this to anyone else in my whole life, Gordon."

"I am greatly honored," I said. "You can trust me completely."

He turned his head, fixing me with pale eyes. The eyes were large and wet and ox-like, and they were so near to me that I could see my own face reflected upside down in the center of each.

"I am now about to let you in on the three best ways in the world of poaching a pheasant," he said. "And seeing that you're the guest on this little trip, I am going to give you the choice of which one you'd like us to use tonight. How's that?"

"There's a catch in this."

"There's no catch, Gordon. I swear it."

"All right, go on."

"Now, here's the thing," he said. "Here's the first big secret." He paused and took a long suck at his cigarette. "Pheasants," he whispered softly, "is *crazy* about raisins."

"Raisins?"

"Just ordinary raisins. It's like a mania with them. My dad discovered that more than forty years ago just like he discovered all three of these methods I'm about to describe to you now."

"I thought you said your dad was a drunk."

"Maybe he was. But he was also a great poacher, Gordon. Possibly the greatest there's ever been in the history of England. My dad studied poaching like a scientist."

"Is that so?"

"I mean it. I really mean it."

"I believe you."

"Do you know," he said, "my dad used to keep a whole flock of prime cockerels in the backyard purely for experimental purposes."

"Cockerels?"

"That's right. And whenever he thought up some new stunt for catching a pheasant, he'd try it out on a cockerel first to see how it worked. That's how he discovered about raisins. It's also how he invented the horsehair method."

Claud paused and glanced over his shoulder as though to make sure that there was nobody listening. "Here's how it's done," he said. "First you take a few raisins and you soak them overnight in water to make them nice and plump and juicy. Then you get a bit of good stiff horsehair and you cut it up into half-inch lengths. Then you push one of these lengths of horsehair through the middle of each raisin so that there's about an eighth of an inch of it sticking out on either side. You follow?"

"Yes."

"Now—the old pheasant comes along and eats one of these raisins. Right? And you're watching him from behind a tree. So what then?"

"I imagine it sticks in his throat."

"That's obvious, Gordon. But here's the amazing thing. Here's what my dad discovered. The moment this happens, the bird *never moves his feet again*! He becomes absolutely rooted to the spot, and there he stands pumping his silly neck up and down just like it was a piston, and all you've got to do is walk calmly out from the place where you're hiding and pick him up in your hands."

"I don't believe that."

"I swear it," he said. "Once a pheasant's had the horsehair you can fire a rifle in his ear and he won't even jump. It's just one of those unexplainable little things. But it takes a genius to discover it."

He paused, and there was a gleam of pride in his eye now as he dwelt for a moment or two upon the memory of his father, the great inventor.

"So that's Method Number One," he said. "Method Number Two is even more simple still. All you do is you have a fishing line. Then you bait the hook with a raisin and you fish for the pheasant just like you fish for a fish. You pay out the line about fifty yards and you lie there on your stomach in the bushes waiting till you get a bite. Then you haul him in."

"I don't think your father invented that one."

"It's very popular with fishermen," he said, choosing not to hear me. "Keen fishermen who can't get down to the seaside as often as they want. It gives them a bit of the old thrill. The only trouble is it's rather noisy. The pheasant squawks like hell as you haul him in, and then every keeper in the wood comes running."

"What is Method Number Three?" I asked.

"Ah," he said. "Number Three's a real beauty. It was the last one my dad ever invented before he passed away."

"His final great work?"

"Exactly, Gordon. And I can even remember the very day it happened, a Sunday morning it was, and suddenly my dad comes into the kitchen holding a huge white cockerel in his hands and he says, 'I think I've got it!' There's a little smile on his face and a shine of glory in his eyes and he comes in very soft and quiet and he puts the bird down right in the middle of the kitchen table and he says, 'By God, I think I've got a good one this time!' 'A good what?' Mum says, looking up from the sink. 'Horace, take that filthy bird off my table.' The cockerel has a funny little paper hat over its head, like an ice-cream cone upside down, and my dad is pointing to it proudly. 'Stroke him,' he says. 'He won't move an inch.' The cockerel starts scratching away at the paper hat with one of its feet, but the hat seems to be stuck on with glue and it won't come off. 'No bird in the world is going to run away once you cover up his eyes,' my dad says, and he starts poking the cockerel with his finger and pushing it around on the table, but it doesn't take the slightest bit of notice. 'You can have this one,' he says, talking to Mum. 'You can kill it and dish it up for dinner as a celebration of what I have just invented.' And then straight away he takes me by the arm and marches me quickly out the door and off we go over the fields and up into the big forest the other side of Haddenham which used to belong to the Duke of Buckingham, and in less than two hours we get five lovely fat pheasants with no more trouble than it takes to go out and buy them in a shop."

Claud paused for breath. His eyes were huge and moist and dreamy as they gazed back into the wonderful world of his youth.

"I don't quite follow this," I said. "How did he get the paper hats over the pheasants' heads up in the woods?"

"You'd never guess it."

"I'm sure I wouldn't."

"Then here it is. First of all you dig a little hole in the ground. Then you twist a piece of paper into the shape of a cone and you fit this into the hole, hollow end upward, like a cup. Then you smear the paper cup all around the inside with birdlime and drop in a few raisins. At the same time you lay a trail of raisins along the ground leading up to it. Now—the old pheasant comes pecking along the trail, and when he gets to the hole he pops his head inside to gobble the raisins and the next thing he knows he's got a paper hat stuck over his eyes and he can't see a thing. Isn't it marvelous what some people think of, Gordon? Don't you agree?"

"Your dad was a genius," I said.

"Then take your pick. Choose whichever one of the three methods you fancy and we'll use it tonight."

"You don't think they're all just a trifle on the crude side, do you?"

"Crude!" he cried, aghast. "Oh my God! And who's been having roasted pheasant in the house nearly every single day for the last six months and not a penny to pay?"

He turned and walked away towards the door of the workshop. I could see that he was deeply pained by my remark.

"Wait a minute," I said. "Don't go."

"You want to come or don't you?"

"Yes, but let me ask you something first. I've just had a bit of an idea."

"Keep it," he said. "You are talking about a subject you don't know the first thing about."

"Do you remember that bottle of sleeping pills the doc gave me last month when I had a bad back?"

"What about them?"

"Is there any reason why those wouldn't work on a pheasant?"

Claud closed his eyes and shook his head pityingly from side to side.

"Wait," I said.

"It's not worth discussing," he said. "No pheasant in the world is going to swallow those lousy red capsules. Don't you know any better than that?"

"You are forgetting the raisins," I said. "Now listen to this. We take a raisin. Then we soak it till it swells. Then we make a tiny slit in one side of it with a razor blade. Then we hollow it out a little. Then we open up one of my red capsules and pour all the powder into the raisin. Then we get a needle and cotton and very carefully we sew up the slit. Now . . ."

Out of the corner of my eye, I saw Claud's mouth slowly beginning to open.

"Now," I said. "We have a nice clean-looking raisin with two and a half grains of seconal inside it, and let me tell *you* something now. That's enough dope to knock the average *man* unconscious, never mind about *birds*!"

I paused for ten seconds to allow the full impact of this to strike home.

"What's more, with this method we could operate on a really grand scale. We could prepare *twenty* raisins if we felt like it, and all we'd have to do is scatter them around the feeding grounds at sunset and then walk away. Half an hour later we'd come back, and the pills would be beginning to work, and the pheasants would be up in the trees by then, roosting, and they'd be starting to feel groggy, and they'd be wobbling and trying to keep their balance, and soon every pheasant that had eaten *one single raisin* would keel over unconscious and fall to the ground. My dear boy, they'd be dropping out of the trees like apples, and all we'd have to do is walk around picking them up!"

Claud was staring at me, rapt.

"Oh Christ," he said softly.

"And they'd never catch us either. We'd simply stroll through the woods dropping a few raisins here and there as we went, and even if they were *watching* us they wouldn't notice anything."

"Gordon," he said, laying a hand on my knee and gazing at me with eyes large and bright as two stars. "If this thing works, it will *revolutionize* poaching."

"I'm glad to hear it."

"How many pills have you got left?" he asked.

"Forty-nine. There were fifty in the bottle and I've only used one."

"Forty-nine's not enough. We want at least two hundred."

"Are you mad!" I cried.

He walked slowly away and stood by the door with his back to me, gazing at the sky.

"Two hundred's the bare minimum," he said quietly. "There's really not much point in doing it unless we have two hundred."

What is it now, I wondered. What the hell's he trying to do?

"This is the last chance we'll have before the season opens," he said.

"I couldn't possibly get any more."

"You wouldn't want us to come back empty-handed, would you?"

"But why so *many*?"

Claud turned his head and looked at me with large innocent eyes. "Why not?" he said gently. "Do you have any objection?"

My God, I thought suddenly. The crazy bastard is out to wreck Mr. Victor Hazel's opening-day shooting party.

"You get us two hundred of those pills," he said, "and then it'll be worth doing."

"I can't."

"You could try, couldn't you?"

Mr. Hazel's party took place on the first of October every year and it was a very famous event. Debilitated gentlemen in tweed suits, some with titles and some who were merely rich, motored in from miles around with their gun-bearers and dogs and wives, and all day long the noise of shooting rolled across the valley. There were always enough pheasants to go round, for each summer the woods were methodically restocked with dozens and dozens of young birds at incredible expense. I had heard it said that the cost of rearing and keeping each pheasant up to the time when it was ready to be shot was well over five pounds (which is approximately the price of two hundred loaves of bread). But to Mr. Hazel it was worth every penny of it. He became, if only for a few hours, a big cheese in a little world and even the Lord Lieutenant of the county slapped him on the back and tried to remember his first name when he said good-bye.

"How would it be if we just reduced the dose?" Claud asked. "Why couldn't we divide the contents of one capsule among four raisins?"

"I suppose you could if you wanted to."

"But would a quarter of a capsule be strong enough for each bird?"

One simply had to admire the man's nerve. It was dangerous enough to poach a single pheasant up in those woods at this time of year and here he was planning to knock off the bloody lot.

"A quarter would be plenty," I said.

"You're sure of that?"

"Work it out for yourself. It's all done by body weight. You'd still be giving about twenty times more than is necessary."

"Then we'll quarter the dose," he said, rubbing his hands. He paused and calculated for a moment. "We'll have one hundred and ninety-six raisins!"

"Do you realize what that involves?" I said. "They'll take hours to prepare."

"What of it!" he cried. "We'll go tomorrow instead. We'll soak the raisins overnight and then we'll have all morning and afternoon to get them ready."

And that was precisely what we did.

Now, twenty-four hours later, we were on our way. We had been walking steadily for about forty minutes and we were nearing the point where the lane curved round to the right and ran along the crest of the hill towards the big wood where the pheasants lived. There was about a mile to go.

"I don't suppose by any chance these keepers might be carrying guns?" I asked.

"All keepers carry guns," Claud said.

I had been afraid of that.

"It's for the vermin mostly."

"Ah."

"Of course there's no guarantee they won't take a pot at a poacher now and again."

"You're joking."

"Not at all. But they only do it from behind. Only when you're running away. They like to pepper you in the legs at about fifty yards."

"They can't do that!" I cried. "It's a criminal offense!"

"So is poaching," Claud said.

We walked on awhile in silence. The sun was below the high hedge on our right now and the lane was in shadow.

"You can consider yourself lucky this isn't thirty years ago," he went on. "They used to shoot you on sight in those days."

"Do you believe that?"

"I know it," he said. "Many's the night when I was a nipper I've gone into the kitchen and seen my old dad lying face downward on the table and Mum standing over him digging the grapeshot out of his buttocks with a potato knife."

"Stop," I said. "It makes me nervous."

"You believe me, don't you?"

"Yes, I believe you."

"Towards the end he was so covered in tiny little white scars he looked exactly like it was snowing."

"Yes," I said. "All right."

"Poacher's arse, they used to call it," Claud said. "And there wasn't a man in the whole village who didn't have a bit of it one way or another. But my dad was the champion."

"Good luck to him," I said.

"I wish to hell he was here now," Claud said, wistful. "He'd have given anything in the world to be coming with us on this job tonight."

"He could take my place," I said. "Gladly."

We had reached the crest of the hill and now we could see the wood ahead of us, huge and dark with the sun going down behind the trees and little sparks of gold shining through.

"You'd better let me have those raisins," Claud said.

I gave him the bag and he slid it gently into his trouser pocket.

"No talking once we're inside," he said. "Just follow me and try not to go snapping any branches."

Five minutes later we were there. The lane ran right up to the wood itself and then skirted the edge of it for about three hundred yards with only a little hedge between. Claud slipped through the hedge on all fours and I followed.

It was cool and dark inside the wood. No sunlight came in at all.

"This is spooky," I said.

"Ssshh!"

Claud was very tense. He was walking just ahead of me, picking his feet up high and putting them down gently on the moist ground. He kept his head moving all the time, the eyes sweeping slowly from side to side, searching for danger. I tried doing the same, but soon I began to see a keeper behind every tree, so I gave it up.

Then a large patch of sky appeared ahead of us in the roof of the forest and I knew that this must be the clearing. Claud had told me that the clearing was the place where the young birds were introduced into the woods in early July, where they were fed and watered and guarded by the keepers, and where many of them stayed from force of habit until the shooting began.

"There's always plenty of pheasants in the clearing," he had said.

"Keepers too, I suppose."

"Yes, but there's thick bushes all around and that helps."

We were now advancing in a series of quick crouching spurts, running from tree to tree and stopping and waiting and listening and running on again, and then at last we were kneeling safely behind a big clump of alder right on the edge of the clearing and Claud was grinning and nudging me in the ribs and pointing through the branches at the pheasants.

The place was absolutely stiff with birds. There must have been two hundred of them at least strutting around among the tree stumps.

"You see what I mean?" Claud whispered.

It was an astonishing sight, a sort of poacher's dream come true. And how close they were! Some of them were not more than ten paces from where we knelt. The hens were plump and creamy brown and they were so fat their breast feathers almost brushed the ground as they walked. The cocks were slim and beautiful, with long tails and brilliant red patches around the eyes, like scarlet spectacles. I glanced at Claud. His big ox-like face was transfixed in ecstasy. The mouth was slightly open and the eyes had a kind of glazy look about them as they stared at the pheasants.

I believe that all poachers react in roughly the same way as this on sighting game. They are like women who sight large emeralds in a jeweler's window, the only difference being that the women are less dignified in the methods they employ later on to acquire the loot. Poacher's arse is nothing to the punishment that a female is willing to endure.

"Ah-ha," Claud said softly. "You see the keeper?"

"Where?"

"Over the other side, by that big tree. Look carefully."

"My God!"

"It's all right. He can't see *us*."

We crouched close to the ground, watching the keeper. He was a smallish man with a cap on his head and a gun under his arm. He never moved. He was like a little post standing there.

"Let's go," I whispered.

The keeper's face was shadowed by the peak of his cap, but it seemed to me that he was looking directly at us.

"I'm not staying here," I said.

"Hush," Claud said.

Slowly, never taking his eyes from the keeper, he reached into his pocket and brought out a single raisin. He placed it in the palm of his right hand, and then quickly, with a little flick of the wrist, he threw the raisin high into the air. I watched it as it went sailing over the bushes and I saw it land within a yard or so of two hen birds standing together beside an old tree stump. Both birds turned their heads sharply at the drop of the raisin. Then one of them hopped over and made a quick peck at the ground and that must have been it.

I glanced up at the keeper. He hadn't moved.

Claud threw a second raisin into the clearing, then a third, and a fourth, and a fifth.

At this point, I saw the keeper turn away his head in order to survey the wood behind him.

Quick as a flash, Claud pulled the paper bag out of his pocket and tipped a huge pile of raisins into the cup of his right hand.

"Stop," I said.

But with a great sweep of the arm he flung the whole handful high over the bushes into the clearing.

They fell with a soft little patter, like raindrops on dry leaves, and every single pheasant in the place must either have seen them coming or heard them fall. There was a flurry of wings and a rush to find the treasure.

The keeper's head flicked round as though there were a spring inside his neck. The birds were all pecking away madly at the raisins. The keeper took two quick paces forward and for a moment I thought he was going to investigate. But then he stopped, and his face came up and his eyes began traveling slowly around the perimeter of the clearing.

"Follow me," Claud whispered. "And *keep down*." He started crawling away swiftly on all fours, like some kind of a monkey.

I went after him. He had his nose close to the ground and his huge tight buttocks were winking at the sky and it was easy to see now how poacher's arse had come to be an occupational disease among the fraternity.

We went along like this for about a hundred yards.

"Now run," Claud said.

We got to our feet and ran, and a few minutes later we emerged through the hedge into the lovely open safety of the lane.

"It went marvelous," Claud said, breathing heavily. "Didn't it go absolutely marvelous?" The big face was scarlet and glowing with triumph.

"It was a mess," I said.

"What!" he cried.

"Of course it was. We can't possibly go back now. That keeper knows there was someone there."

"He knows nothing," Claud said. "In another five minutes it'll be pitch dark inside the wood and he'll be sloping off home to his supper."

"I think I'll join him."

"You're a great poacher," Claud said. He sat down on the grassy bank under the hedge and lit a cigarette.

The sun had set now and the sky was a pale smoke blue, faintly glazed with yellow. In the woods behind us the shadows and the spaces in between the trees were turning from gray to black.

"How long does a sleeping pill take to work?" Claud asked.

"Look out," I said. "There's someone coming."

The man had appeared suddenly and silently out of the dusk and he was only thirty yards away when I saw him.

"Another bloody keeper," Claud said.

We both looked at the keeper as he came down the lane towards us. He had a shotgun under his arm and there was a black Labrador walking at his heels. He stopped when he was a few paces away and the dog stopped with him and stayed behind him, watching us through the keeper's legs.

"Good evening," Claud said, nice and friendly.

This one was a tall bony man about forty with a swift eye and a hard cheek and hard dangerous hands.

"I know you," he said softly, coming closer. "I know the both of you."

Claud didn't answer this.

"You're from the fillin' station. Right?"

His lips were thin and dry, with some sort of a brownish crust over them.

"You're Cubbage and Hawes and you're from the fillin' station on the main road. Right?"

"What are we playing?" Claud said. "Twenty Questions?"

The keeper spat out a big gob of spit and I saw it go floating through the air and land with a plop on a patch of dry dust six inches from Claud's feet. It looked like a little baby oyster lying there.

"Beat it," the man said. "Go on. Get out."

Claud sat on the bank smoking his cigarette and looking at the gob of spit.

"Go on," the man said. "Get out."

When he spoke, the upper lip lifted above the gum and I could see a row of small discolored teeth, one of them black, the others quince and ocher.

"This happens to be a public highway," Claud said. "Kindly do not molest us."

The keeper shifted the gun from his left arm to his right.

"You're loiterin'," he said, "with intent to commit a felony. I could run you in for that."

"No you couldn't," Claud said.

All this made me rather nervous.

"I've had my eye on you for some time," the keeper said, looking at Claud.

"It's getting late," I said. "Shall we stroll on?"

Claud flipped away his cigarette and got slowly to his feet. "All right," he said. "Let's go."

We wandered off down the lane the way we had come, leaving the keeper standing there, and soon the man was out of sight in the half-darkness behind us.

"That's the head keeper," Claud said. "His name is Rabbetts."

"Let's get the hell out," I said.

"Come in here," Claud said.

There was a gate on our left leading into a field and we climbed over it and sat down behind the hedge.

"Mr. Rabbetts is also due for his supper," Claud said. "You mustn't worry about him."

We sat quietly behind the hedge waiting for the keeper to walk past us on his way home. A few stars were showing and a bright three-quarter moon was coming up over the hills behind us in the east.

"Here he is," Claud whispered. "Don't move."

The keeper came loping softly up the lane with the dog padding quick and soft footed at his heels, and we watched them through the hedge as they went by.

"He won't be coming back tonight," Claud said.

"How do you know that?"

"A keeper never waits for you in the wood if he knows where you live. He goes to your house and hides outside and watches for you to come back."

"That's worse."

"No, it isn't, not if you dump the loot somewhere else before you go home. He can't touch you then."

"What about the other one, the one in the clearing?"

"He's gone too."

"You can't be sure of that."

"I've been studying these bastards for months, Gordon, honest I have. I know all their habits. There's no danger."

Reluctantly I followed him back into the wood. It was pitch dark in there now and very silent, and as we moved cautiously forward the noise of our footsteps seemed to go echoing around the walls of the forest as though we were walking in a cathedral.

"Here's where we threw the raisins," Claud said.

I peered through the bushes.

The clearing lay dim and milky in the moonlight.

"You're quite sure the keeper's gone?"

"I *know* he's gone."

I could just see Claud's face under the peak of his cap, the pale lips, the soft pale cheeks, and the large eyes with a little spark of excitement dancing slowly in each.

"Are they roosting?"

"Yes."

"Whereabouts?"

"All around. They don't go far."

"What do we do next?"

"We stay here and wait. I brought you a light," he added, and he handed me one of those small pocket flashlights shaped like a fountain pen. "You may need it."

I was beginning to feel better. "Shall we see if we can spot some of them sitting in the trees?" I said.

"No."

"I should like to see how they look when they're roosting."

"This isn't a nature study," Claud said. "Please be quiet."

We stood there for a long time waiting for something to happen.

"I've just had a nasty thought," I said. "If a bird can keep its balance on a branch when it's asleep, then surely there isn't any reason why the pills should make it fall down."

Claud looked at me quick.

"After all," I said, "it's not dead. It's still only sleeping."

"It's doped," Claud said.

"But that's just a *deeper* sort of sleep. Why should we expect it to fall down just because it's in a *deeper* sleep?"

There was a gloomy silence.

"We should've tried it with chickens," Claud said. "My dad would've done that."

"Your dad was a genius," I said.

At that moment there came a soft thump from the wood behind us.

"Hey!"

"Sshh!"

We stood listening.

Thump.

"There's another!"

It was a deep muffled sound as though a bag of sand had been dropped from about shoulder height.

Thump!

"They're pheasants!" I cried.

"Wait!"

"I'm sure they're pheasants!"

Thump! Thump!

"You're right!"

We ran back into the wood.

"Where were they?"

"Over here! Two of them were over here!"

"I thought they were this way."

"Keep looking!" Claud shouted. "They can't be far."

We searched for about a minute.

"Here's one!" he called.

When I got to him he was holding a magnificent cock bird in both hands. We examined it closely with our flashlights.

"It's doped to the gills," Claud said. "It's still alive, I can feel its heart, but it's doped to the bloody gills."

Thump!

"There's another!"

Thump! Thump!

"Two more!"

Thump!

Thump! Thump! Thump!

"Jesus Christ!"

Thump! Thump! Thump! Thump!

Thump! Thump!

All around us the pheasants were starting to rain down out of the trees. We began rushing around madly in the dark, sweeping the ground with our flashlights.

Thump! Thump! Thump! This lot fell almost on top of me. I was right under the tree as they came down and I found all three of them immediately—two cocks and a hen. They were limp and warm, the feathers wonderfully soft in the hand.

"Where shall I put them?" I called out. I was holding them by the legs.

"Lay them here, Gordon! Just pile them up here where it's light!"

Claud was standing on the edge of the clearing with the moonlight streaming down all over him and a great bunch of pheasants in each hand. His face was bright, his eyes big and bright and wonderful, and he was staring around him like a child who has just discovered that the whole world is made of chocolate.

Thump!

Thump! Thump!

"I don't like it," I said. "It's too many."

"It's beautiful!" he cried and he dumped the birds he was carrying and ran off to look for more.

Thump! Thump! Thump! Thump!

Thump!

It was easy to find them now. There were one or two lying under every tree. I quickly collected six more, three in each hand, and ran back and dumped them with the others. Then six more. Then six more after that.

And still they kept falling.

Claud was in a whirl of ecstasy now, dashing about like a mad ghost under the trees. I could see the beam of his flashlight waving around in the dark and each time he found a bird he gave a little yelp of triumph.

Thump! Thump! Thump!

"That bugger Hazel ought to hear this!" he called out.

"Don't shout," I said. "It frightens me."

"What's that?"

"Don't *shout.* There might be keepers."

"Screw the keepers!" he cried. "They're all eating!"

For three or four minutes, the pheasants kept on falling. Then suddenly they stopped.

"Keep searching!" Claud shouted. "There's plenty more on the ground!"

"Don't you think we ought to get out while the going's good?"

"No," he said.

We went on searching. Between us we looked under every tree within a hundred yards of the clearing, north, south, east, and west, and I think we found most of them in the end. At the collecting point there was a pile of pheasants as big as a bonfire.

"It's a miracle," Claud was saying. "It's a bloody miracle." He was staring at them in a kind of trance.

"We'd better just take half a dozen each and get out quick," I said.

"I would like to count them, Gordon."

"There's no time for that."

"I must count them."

"No," I said. "Come on."

"One . . .

"Two . . .

"Three . . .

"Four . . .

He began counting them very carefully, picking up each bird in turn and laying it carefully to one side. The moon was directly overhead now and the whole clearing was brilliantly illuminated.

"I'm not standing around here like this," I said. I walked back a few paces and hid myself in the shadows, waiting for him to finish.

"A hundred and seventeen . . . a hundred and eighteen . . . a hundred and nineteen . . . *a hundred and twenty!*" he cried. "*One hundred and twenty birds!* It's an all-time record!"

I didn't doubt it for a moment.

"The most my dad ever got in one night was fifteen and he was drunk for a week afterwards!"

"You're the champion of the world," I said. "Are you ready now?"

"One minute," he answered and he pulled up his sweater and proceeded to unwind the two big white cotton sacks from around his belly. "Here's yours," he said, handing one of them to me. "Fill it up quick."

The light of the moon was so strong I could read the small print along the base of the sack. J. W. CRUMP, it said. KESTON FLOUR MILLS, LONDON SW17.

"You don't think that bastard with the brown teeth is watching us this very moment from behind a tree?"

"There's no chance of that," Claud said. "He's down at the filling station like I told you, waiting for us to come home."

We started loading the pheasants into the sacks. They were soft and floppy necked and the skin underneath the feathers was still warm.

"There'll be a taxi waiting for us in the lane," Claud said.

"What?"

"I always go back in a taxi, Gordon, didn't you know that?"

I told him I didn't.

"A taxi is anonymous," Claud said. "Nobody knows who's inside a taxi except the driver. My dad taught me that."

"Which driver?"

"Charlie Kinch. He's only too glad to oblige."

We finished loading the pheasants, and I tried to hump my bulging sack onto my shoulder. My sack had about sixty birds inside it, and it must have weighed a hundredweight and a half, at least. "I can't carry this," I said. "We'll have to leave some of them behind."

"Drag it," Claud said. "Just pull it behind you."

We started off through the pitch-black woods, pulling the pheasants behind us. "We'll never make it all the way back to the village like this," I said.

"Charlie's never let me down yet," Claud said.

We came to the margin of the wood and peered through the hedge into the lane. Claud said, "Charlie boy," very softly and the old man behind the wheel of the taxi not five yards away poked his head out into the moonlight and gave us a sly toothless grin. We slid through the hedge, dragging the sacks after us along the ground.

"Hullo!" Charlie said. "What's this?"

"It's cabbages," Claud told him. "Open the door."

Two minutes later we were safely inside the taxi, cruising slowly down the hill towards the village.

171

It was all over now bar the shouting. Claud was triumphant, bursting with pride and excitement, and he kept leaning forward and tapping Charlie Kinch on the shoulder and saying, "How about it, Charlie? How about this for a haul?" and Charlie kept glancing back pop-eyed at the huge bulging sacks lying on the floor between us and saying, "Jesus Christ, man, how did you do it?"

"There's six brace of them for you, Charlie," Claud said. And Charlie said, "I reckon pheasants is going to be a bit scarce up at Mr. Victor Hazel's opening-day shoot this year," and Claud said, "I imagine they are, Charlie, I imagine they are."

"What in God's name are you going to do with a hundred and twenty pheasants?" I asked.

"Put them in cold storage for the winter," Claud said. "Put them in with the dog meat in the deep freeze at the filling station."

"Not tonight, I trust?"

"No, Gordon, not tonight. We leave them at Bessie's house tonight."

"Bessie who?"

"Bessie Organ."

"Bessie *Organ*!"

"Bessie always delivers my game, didn't you know that?"

"I don't know anything," I said. I was completely stunned. Mrs. Organ was the wife of the Reverend Jack Organ, the local vicar.

"Always choose a respectable woman to deliver your game," Claud announced. "That's correct, Charlie, isn't it?"

"Bessie's a right smart girl," Charlie said.

We were driving through the village now and the streetlamps were still on and the men were wandering home from the pubs. I saw Will Prattley letting himself in quietly by the side door of his fishmonger's shop and Mrs. Prattley's head was sticking out of the window just above him, but he didn't know it.

"The vicar is very partial to roasted pheasant," Claud said.

"He hangs it eighteen days," Charlie said, "then he gives it a couple of good shakes and all the feathers drop off."

The taxi turned left and swung in through the gates of the vicarage. There were no lights on in the house and nobody met us. Claud and I dumped the pheasants in the coal shed at the rear, and then we said good-bye to Charlie Kinch and walked back in the moonlight to the filling station, empty-handed. Whether or not Mr. Rabbetts was watching us as we went in, I do not know. We saw no sign of him.

"Here she comes," Claud said to me the next morning.

"Who?"

"Bessie—Bessie Organ." He spoke the name proudly and with a slight proprietary air, as though he were a general referring to his bravest officer.

I followed him outside.

"Down there," he said, pointing.

Far away down the road I could see a small female figure advancing towards us.

"What's she pushing?" I asked.

Claud gave me a sly look.

"There's only one safe way of delivering game," he announced, "and that's under a baby."

"Yes," I murmured, "yes, of course."

"That'll be young Christopher Organ in there, aged one and a half. He's a lovely child, Gordon."

I could just make out the small dot of a baby sitting high up in the pram, which had its hood folded down.

"There's sixty or seventy pheasants at least under that little nipper," Claud said happily. "You just imagine that."

"You can't put sixty or seventy pheasants in a pram."

"You can if it's got a deep well underneath it, and if you take out the mattress and pack them in tight, right up to the top. All you need then is a sheet. You'll be surprised how little room a pheasant takes up when it's limp."

We stood beside the pumps waiting for Bessie Organ to arrive. It was one of those warm windless September mornings with a darkening sky and a smell of thunder in the air.

"Right through the village bold as brass," Claud said. "Good old Bessie."

"She seems in rather a hurry to me."

Claud lit a new cigarette from the stub of the old one. "Bessie is never in a hurry," he said.

"She certainly isn't walking normal," I told him. "You look."

He squinted at her through the smoke of his cigarette. Then he took the cigarette out of his mouth and looked again.

"Well?" I said.

"She does seem to be going a tiny bit quick, doesn't she?" he said carefully.

"She's going damn quick."

There was a pause. Claud was beginning to stare very hard at the approaching woman.

"Perhaps she doesn't want to be caught in the rain, Gordon. I'll bet that's exactly what it is, she thinks it's going to rain and she don't want the baby to get wet."

"Why doesn't she put the hood up?"

He didn't answer this.

"She's *running*!" Claud cried. "Look!" Bessie had suddenly broken into a full sprint.

Claud stood very still, watching the woman; and in the silence that followed I fancied I could hear a baby screaming.

"What's up?"

He didn't answer.

"There's something wrong with that baby," I said. "Listen."

At this point, Bessie was about two hundred yards away from us but closing fast.

"Can you hear him now?" I said.

"Yes."

"He's yelling his head off."

The small shrill voice in the distance was growing louder every second, frantic, piercing, nonstop, almost hysterical.

"He's having a fit," Claud announced.

"I think he must be."

"That's why she's running, Gordon. She wants to get him in here quick and put him under a cold tap."

"I'm sure you're right," I said. "In fact I know you're right. Just listen to that noise."

"If it isn't a fit, you can bet your life it's something like it."

"I quite agree."

Claud shifted his feet uneasily on the gravel of the driveway.

"There's a thousand and one different things keep happening every day to little babies like that," he said.

"Of course."

"I knew a baby once who caught his fingers in the spokes of the pram wheel. He lost the lot. It cut them clean off."

"Yes."

"Whatever it is," Claud said, "I wish to Christ she'd stop running."

A long truck loaded with bricks came up behind Bessie and the driver slowed down and poked his head out of the window to stare. Bessie ignored him and flew on, and she was so close now I could see her big red face with the mouth wide open, panting for breath. I noticed she was wearing white gloves on her hands, very prim and dainty, and there was a funny little white hat to match perched right on the top of her head, like a mushroom.

Suddenly, out of the pram, straight up into the air, flew an enormous pheasant!

Claud let out a cry of horror.

The fool in the truck going along beside Bessie started roaring with laughter.

The pheasant flapped around drunkenly for a few seconds, then it lost height and landed in the grass by the side of the road.

A grocer's van came up behind the truck and began hooting to get by. Bessie kept running.

Then—*whoosh!*—a second pheasant flew up out of the pram.

Then a third, and a fourth. Then a fifth.

"My God!" I said. "It's the pills! They're wearing off!"

Claud didn't say anything.

Bessie covered the last fifty yards at a tremendous pace, and she came swinging into the driveway of the filling station with birds flying up out of the pram in all directions.

"What the hell's going on?" she cried.

"Go round the back!" I shouted. "Go round the back!" But she pulled up sharp against the first pump in the line, and before we could reach her she had seized the screaming infant in her arms and dragged him clear.

"No! No!" Claud cried, racing towards her. "Don't lift the baby! Put him back! Hold down the sheet!" But she wasn't even listening, and with the weight of the child suddenly lifted away, a great cloud of pheasants rose up out of the pram, fifty or sixty of them, at least, and the whole sky above us was filled with huge brown birds flapping their wings furiously to gain height.

Claud and I started running up and down the driveway waving our arms to frighten them off the premises. "Go away!" we shouted. "Shoo! Go away!" But they were too dopey still to take any notice of us and within half a minute down they came again and settled themselves like a swarm of locusts all over the front of my filling station. The place was covered with them. They sat wing to wing along the edges of the roof and on the concrete canopy that came out over the pumps, and a dozen at least were clinging to the sill of the office window. Some had flown down on to the rack that held the bottles of lubricating oil, and others were sliding about on the bonnets of my secondhand cars. One cock bird with a fine tail was perched superbly on top of a petrol pump, and quite a number, those that were too drunk to stay aloft, simply squatted in the driveway at our feet, fluffing their feathers and blinking their small eyes.

Across the road, a line of cars had already started forming behind the brick lorry and the grocery van, and people were opening their doors and getting out and beginning to cross over to have a closer look. I glanced at my watch. It was twenty to nine. Any moment now, I thought, a large black car is going to come streaking along the road from the direction of the village, and the car will be a Rolls, and the face behind the wheel will be the great glistening brewer's face of Mr. Victor Hazel.

"They near pecked him to pieces!" Bessie was shouting, clasping the screaming baby to her bosom.

"You go on home, Bessie," Claud said, white in the face.

"Lock up," I said. "Put out the sign. We've gone for the day."

Beware of the Dog

Down below there was only a vast white undulating sea of cloud. Above there was the sun, and the sun was white like the clouds, because it is never yellow when one looks at it from high in the air.

He was still flying the Spitfire. His right hand was on the stick and he was working the rudder bar with his left leg alone. It was quite easy. The machine was flying well. He knew what he was doing.

Everything is fine, he thought. I'm doing all right. I'm doing nicely. I know my way home. I'll be there in half an hour. When I land I shall taxi in and switch off my engine and I shall say, help me to get out, will you. I shall make my voice sound ordinary and natural and none of them will take any notice. Then I shall say, someone help me to get out. I can't do it alone because I've lost one of my legs. They'll all laugh and think that I'm joking and I shall say, all right, come and have a look, you unbelieving bastards. Then Yorky will climb up on to the wing and look inside. He'll probably be sick because of all the blood and the mess. I shall laugh and say, for God's sake, help me get out.

He glanced down again at his right leg. There was not much of it left. The cannon shell had taken him on the thigh, just above the knee, and now there was nothing but a great mess and a lot of blood. But

179

there was no pain. When he looked down, he felt as though he were seeing something that did not belong to him. It had nothing to do with him. It was just a mess which happened to be there in the cockpit; something strange and unusual and rather interesting. It was like finding a dead cat on the sofa.

He really felt fine, and because he still felt fine, he felt excited and unafraid.

I won't even bother to call up on the radio for the blood wagon, he thought. It isn't necessary. And when I land I'll sit there quite normally and say, some of you fellows come and help me out, will you, because I've lost one of my legs. That will be funny. I'll laugh a little while I'm saying it; I'll say it calmly and slowly, and they'll think I'm joking. When Yorky comes up on to the wing and gets sick, I'll say, Yorky you old son of a bitch, have you fixed my car yet? Then when I get out I'll make my report. Later I'll go up to London. I'll take that half bottle of whiskey with me and I'll give it to Bluey. We'll sit in her room and drink it. I'll get the water out of the bathroom tap. I won't say much until it's time to go to bed, then I'll say, Bluey, I've got a surprise for you. I lost a leg today. But I don't mind so long as you don't. It doesn't even hurt. We'll go everywhere in cars. I always hated walking except when I walked down the street of the coppersmiths in Baghdad, but I could go in a rickshaw. I could go home and chop wood, but the head always flies off the ax. Hot water, that's what it needs; put it in the bath and make the handle swell. I chopped lots of wood last time I went home and I put the ax in the bath . . .

Then he saw the sun shining on the engine cowling of his machine. He saw the sun shining on the rivets in the metal, and he remembered the airplane and he remembered where he was. He realized that he was no longer feeling good; that he was sick and giddy. His head kept falling forward on to his chest because his neck seemed no longer to have any strength. But he knew that he was flying the Spitfire. He could feel the handle of the stick between the fingers of his right hand.

I'm going to pass out, he thought. Any moment now I'm going to pass out.

He looked at his altimeter. Twenty-one thousand. To test himself he tried to read the hundreds as well as the thousands. Twenty-one thousand and what? As he looked the dial became blurred and he could not even see the needle. He knew then that he must bale out; that there was not a second to lose, otherwise he would become unconscious. Quickly, frantically, he tried to slide back the hood with his left hand, but he had not the strength. For a second he took his right hand off the stick and with both hands he managed to push the hood back. The rush of cold air on his face seemed to help. He had a moment of great clearness. His actions became orderly and precise. That is what happens with a good pilot. He took some quick deep breaths from his oxygen mask, and as he did so, he looked out over the side of the cockpit. Down below there was only a vast white sea of cloud and he realized that he did not know where he was.

It'll be the Channel, he thought. I'm sure to fall in the drink.

He throttled back, pulled off his helmet, undid his straps, and pushed the stick hard over to the left. The Spitfire dipped its port wing and turned smoothly over on to its back. The pilot fell out.

As he fell, he opened his eyes, because he knew that he must not pass out before he had pulled the cord. On one side he saw the sun; on the other he saw the whiteness of the clouds, and as he fell, as he somersaulted in the air, the white clouds chased the sun and the sun chased the clouds. They chased each other in a small circle; they ran faster and faster and there was the sun and the clouds and the clouds and the sun, and the clouds came nearer until suddenly there was no longer any sun but only a great whiteness. The whole world was white and there was nothing in it. It was so white that sometimes it looked black, and after a time it was either white or black, but mostly it was white. He watched it as it turned from white to black, then back to white again, and the white stayed for a long time, but the black lasted only for a few seconds. He got into the habit of going to sleep during the white periods, of waking up just in time to see the world when it was black. The black was very quick. Sometimes it was only a flash, a flash of black lightning. The white was slow and in the slowness of it, he always dozed off.

One day, when it was white, he put out a hand and he touched something. He took it between his fingers and crumpled it. For a time he lay there, idly letting the tips of his fingers play with the thing which they had touched. Then slowly he opened his eyes, looked down at his hand and saw that he was holding something which was white. It was the edge of a sheet. He knew it was a sheet because he could see the texture of the material and the stitchings on the hem. He screwed up his eyes and opened them again quickly. This time he saw the room. He saw the bed in which he was lying: he saw the gray walls and the door and the green curtains over the window. There were some roses on the table by his bed.

Then he saw the basin on the table near the roses. It was a white enamel basin and beside it there was a small medicine glass.

This is a hospital, he thought. I am in a hospital. But he could remember nothing. He lay back on his pillow, looking at the ceiling and wondering what had happened. He was gazing at the smooth grayness of the ceiling which was so clean and gray, and then suddenly he saw a fly walking upon it. The sight of this fly, the suddenness of seeing this small black speck on a sea of gray, brushed the surface of his brain, and quickly, in that second, he remembered everything. He remembered the Spitfire and he remembered the altimeter showing twenty-one thousand feet. He remembered the pushing back of the hood with both hands and he remembered the baling out. He remembered his leg.

It seemed all right now. He looked down at the end of the bed, but he could not tell. He put one hand underneath the bedclothes and felt for his knees. He found one of them, but when he felt for the other, his hand touched something which was soft and covered in bandages.

Just then the door opened and a nurse came in.

"Hullo," she said. "So you've woken up at last."

She was not good-looking, but she was large and clean. She was between thirty and forty and she had fair hair. More than that he did not notice.

"Where am I?"

"You're a lucky fellow. You landed in a wood near the beach. You're in Brighton. They brought you in two days ago, and now you're all fixed up. You look fine."

"I've lost a leg," he said.

"That's nothing. We'll get you another one. Now you must go to sleep. The doctor will be coming to see you in about an hour." She picked up the basin and the medicine glass and went out.

But he did not sleep. He wanted to keep his eyes open because he was frightened that if he shut them again everything would go away. He lay looking at the ceiling. The fly was still there. It was very ener-

getic. It would run forward very fast for a few inches, then it would
stop. Then it would run forward again, stop, run forward, and every
now and then it would take off and buzz around viciously in small cir-
cles. It always landed back in the same place on the ceiling and started
running and stopping all over again. He watched it for so long that after a while it was no longer a fly, but only a black speck upon a sea of
gray, and he was still watching it when the nurse opened the door, and
stood aside while the doctor came in. He was an Army doctor, a major,
and he had some last war ribbons on his chest. He was bald and small,
but he had a cheerful face and kind eyes.

"Well, well," he said. "So you've decided to wake up at last. How are
you feeling?"

"I feel all right."

"That's the stuff. You'll be up and about in no time."

The doctor took his wrist to feel his pulse.

"By the way," he said, "some of the lads from your squadron were
ringing up and asking about you. They wanted to come along and see
you, but I said that they'd better wait a day or two. Told them you were
all right and that they could come and see you a little later on. Just lie
quiet and take it easy for a bit. Got something to read?" He glanced at
the table with the roses. "No. Well, nurse will look after you. She'll get
you anything you want." With that he waved his hand and went out,
followed by the large clean nurse.

When they had gone, he lay back and looked at the ceiling again.
The fly was still there and as he lay watching it he heard the noise of an
airplane in the distance. He lay listening to the sound of its engines. It
was a long way away. I wonder what it is, he thought. Let me see if I
can place it. Suddenly he jerked his head sharply to one side. Anyone

who has been bombed can tell the noise of a Junkers 88. They can tell most other German bombers for that matter, but especially a Junkers 88. The engines seem to sing a duet. There is a deep vibrating bass voice and with it there is a high-pitched tenor. It is the singing of the tenor which makes the sound of a Ju-88 something which one cannot mistake.

He lay listening to the noise and he felt quite certain about what it was. But where were the sirens and where the guns? That German pilot certainly had a nerve coming near Brighton alone in daylight.

The aircraft was always far away and soon the noise faded away into the distance. Later on there was another. This one, too, was far away, but there was the same deep undulating bass and the high swinging tenor and there was no mistaking it. He had heard that noise every day during the battle.

He was puzzled. There was a bell on the table by the bed. He reached out his hand and rang it. He heard the noise of footsteps down the corridor. The nurse came in.

"Nurse, what were those airplanes?"

"I'm sure I don't know. I didn't hear them. Probably fighters or bombers. I expect they were returning from France. Why, what's the matter?"

"They were Ju-88s. I'm sure they were Ju-88s. I know the sound of the engines. There were two of them. What were they doing over here?"

The nurse came up to the side of his bed and began to straighten out the sheets and tuck them in under the mattress.

"Gracious me, what things you imagine. You mustn't worry about a thing like that. Would you like me to get you something to read?"

"No, thank you."

She patted his pillow and brushed back the hair from his forehead with her hand.

"They never come over in daylight any longer. You know that. They were probably Lancasters or Flying Fortresses."

"Nurse."

"Yes."

"Could I have a cigarette?"

"Why, certainly you can."

She went out and came back almost at once with a packet of Players and some matches. She handed one to him and when he had put it in his mouth, she struck a match and lit it.

"If you want me again," she said, "just ring the bell," and she went out.

Once towards evening he heard the noise of another aircraft. It was far away, but even so he knew that it was a single-engined machine. It was going fast; he could tell that. He could not place it. It wasn't a Spit, and it wasn't a Hurricane. It did not sound like an American engine either. They make more noise. He did not know what it was, and it worried him greatly. Perhaps I am very ill, he thought. Perhaps I am imagining things. Perhaps I am a little delirious. I simply do not know what to think.

That evening the nurse came in with a basin of hot water and began to wash him.

"Well," she said, "I hope you don't think that we're being bombed."

She had taken off his pajama top and was soaping his right arm with a flannel. He did not answer.

She rinsed the flannel in the water, rubbed more soap on it, and began to wash his chest.

"You're looking fine this evening," she said. "They operated on you as soon as you came in. They did a marvelous job. You'll be all right. I've got a brother in the RAF," she added. "Flying bombers."

He said, "I went to school in Brighton."

She looked up quickly. "Well, that's fine," she said. "I expect you'll know some people in the town."

"Yes," he said, "I know quite a few."

She had finished washing his chest and arms. Now she turned back the bedclothes so that his left leg was uncovered. She did it in such a way that his bandaged stump remained under the sheets. She undid the cord of his pajama trousers and took them off. There was no trouble because they had cut off the right trouser leg so that it could not interfere with the bandages. She began to wash his left leg and the rest of his body. This was the first time he had had a bed bath and he was embarrassed. She laid a towel under his leg and began washing his foot with the flannel. She said, "This wretched soap won't lather at all. It's the water. It's as hard as nails."

He said, "None of the soap is very good now and, of course, with hard water it's hopeless." As he said it he remembered something. He remembered the baths which he used to take at school in Brighton, in the long stone-floored bathroom which had four baths in a row. He remembered how the water was so soft that you had to take a shower afterwards to get all the soap off your body, and he remembered how the foam used to float on the surface of the water, so that you could not see your legs underneath. He remembered that sometimes they were given calcium tablets because the school doctor used to say that soft water was bad for the teeth.

"In Brighton," he said, "the water isn't . . ."

He did not finish the sentence. Something had occurred to him; something so fantastic and absurd that for a moment he felt like telling the nurse about it and having a good laugh.

She looked up. "The water isn't what?" she said.

"Nothing," he answered. "I was dreaming."

She rinsed the flannel in the basin, wiped the soap off his leg and dried him with a towel.

"It's nice to be washed," he said. "I feel better." He was feeling his face with his hand. "I need a shave."

"We'll do that tomorrow," she said. "Perhaps you can do it yourself then."

That night he could not sleep. He lay awake thinking of the Junkers 88s and of the hardness of the water. He could think of nothing else. They were Ju-88s, he said to himself. I know they were. And yet it is not possible, because they would not be flying around so low over here in broad daylight. I know that it is true and yet I know that it is impossible. Perhaps I am ill. Perhaps I am behaving like a fool and do not know what I am doing or saying. Perhaps I am delirious. For a long time he lay awake thinking these things, and once he sat up in bed and said aloud, "I will prove that I am not crazy. I will make a little speech about something complicated and intellectual. I will talk about what to do with Germany after the war." But before he had time to begin, he was asleep.

He woke just as the first light of day was showing through the slit in the curtains over the window. The room was still dark, but he could tell that it was already beginning to get light outside. He lay looking at the gray light which was showing through the slit in the curtain and as he lay there he remembered the day before. He remembered the Junkers 88s and the hardness of the water; he remembered the large pleasant nurse and the kind doctor, and now a small grain of doubt took root in his mind and it began to grow.

He looked around the room. The nurse had taken the roses out the night before. There was nothing except the table with a packet of cigarettes, a box of matches and an ashtray. The room was bare. It was no longer warm or friendly. It was not even comfortable. It was cold and empty and very quiet.

Slowly the grain of doubt grew, and with it came fear, a light, dancing fear that warned but did not frighten; the kind of fear that one gets not because one is afraid, but because one feels that there is something wrong. Quickly the doubt and the fear grew so that he became restless and angry, and when he touched his forehead with his hand, he found that it was damp with sweat. He knew then that he must do something; that he must find some way of proving to himself that he was either right or wrong, and he looked up and saw again the window and the green curtains. From where he lay, that window was right in front of him, but it was fully ten yards away. Somehow he must reach it and look out. The idea became an obsession with him and soon he could think of nothing except the window. But what about his leg? He put his hand underneath the bedclothes and felt the thick bandaged stump which was all that was left on the right-hand side. It seemed all right. It didn't hurt. But it would not be easy.

He sat up. Then he pushed the bedclothes aside and put his left leg on the floor. Slowly, carefully, he swung his body over until he had both

189

hands on the floor as well; then he was out of bed, kneeling on the carpet. He looked at the stump. It was very short and thick, covered with bandages. It was beginning to hurt and he could feel it throbbing. He wanted to collapse, lie down on the carpet and do nothing, but he knew that he must go on.

With two arms and one leg, he crawled over towards the window. He would reach forward as far as he could with his arms, then he would give a little jump and slide his left leg along after them. Each time he did it, it jarred his wound so that he gave a soft grunt of pain, but he continued to crawl across the floor on two hands and one knee. When he got to the window he reached up, and one at a time he placed both hands on the sill. Slowly he raised himself up until he was standing on his left leg. Then quickly he pushed aside the curtains and looked out.

He saw a small house with a gray tiled roof standing alone beside a narrow lane, and immediately behind it there was a plowed field. In front of the house there was an untidy garden, and there was a green hedge separating the garden from the lane. He was looking at the hedge when he saw the sign. It was just a piece of board nailed to the top of a short pole, and because the hedge had not been trimmed for a long time, the branches had grown out around the sign so that it seemed almost as though it had been placed in the middle of the hedge. There was something written on the board with white paint. He pressed his head against the glass of the window, trying to read what it said. The first letter was a G, he could see that. The second was an A, and the third was an R. One after another he managed to see what the letters were. There were three words, and slowly he spelled the letters out aloud to himself as he managed to read them. G-A-R-D-E A-U C-H-I-E-N, *Garde au chien.* That is what it said.

He stood there balancing on one leg and holding tightly to the edges of the windowsill with his hands, staring at the sign and at the whitewashed lettering of the words. For a moment he could think of nothing at all. He stood there looking at the sign, repeating the words over and over to himself. Slowly he began to realize the full meaning of the thing. He looked up at the cottage and at the plowed field. He looked at the small orchard on the left of the cottage and he looked at the green countryside beyond. "So this is France," he said. "I am in France."

Now the throbbing in his right thigh was very great. It felt as though someone was pounding the end of his stump with a hammer and suddenly the pain became so intense that it affected his head. For a moment he thought he was going to fall. Quickly he knelt down again, crawled back to the bed and hoisted himself in. He pulled the bedclothes over himself and lay back on the pillow, exhausted. He could still think of nothing at all except the small sign by the hedge and the plowed field and the orchard. It was the words on the sign that he could not forget.

It was some time before the nurse came in. She came carrying a basin of hot water and she said, "Good morning, how are you today?"

He said, "Good morning, nurse."

The pain was still great under the bandages, but he did not wish to tell this woman anything. He looked at her as she busied herself with getting the washing things ready. He looked at her more carefully now. Her hair was very fair. She was tall and big boned and her face seemed pleasant. But there was something a little uneasy about her eyes. They were never still. They never looked at anything for more than a moment and they moved too quickly from one place to another in the room. There was something about her movements also. They were too sharp and nervous to go well with the casual manner in which she spoke.

She set down the basin, took off his pajama top, and began to wash him.

"Did you sleep well?"

"Yes."

"Good," she said. She was washing his arms and his chest.

"I believe there's someone coming down to see you from the Air Ministry after breakfast," she went on. "They want a report or something. I expect you know all about it. How you got shot down and all that. I won't let him stay long, so don't worry."

He did not answer. She finished washing him and gave him a toothbrush and some toothpowder. He brushed his teeth, rinsed his mouth and spat the water out into the basin.

Later she brought him his breakfast on a tray, but he did not want to eat. He was still feeling weak and sick, and he wished only to lie still and think about what had happened. And there was a sentence running through his head. It was a sentence which Johnny, the Intelligence Officer of his squadron, always repeated to the pilots every day before they went out. He could see Johnny now, leaning against the wall of the dispersal hut with his pipe in his hand, saying, "And if they get you, don't forget, just your name, rank, and number. Nothing else. For God's sake, say nothing else."

"There you are," she said as she put the tray on his lap. "I've got you an egg. Can you manage all right?"

"Yes."

She stood beside the bed. "Are you feeling all right?"

"Yes."

"Good. If you want another egg I might be able to get you one."

"This is all right."

"Well, just ring the bell if you want any more." And she went out.

He had just finished eating, when the nurse came in again.

She said, "Wing Commander Roberts is here. I've told him that he can only stay for a few minutes."

She beckoned with her hand and the Wing Commander came in.

"Sorry to bother you like this," he said.

He was an ordinary RAF officer, dressed in a uniform which was a little shabby. He wore wings and a DFC. He was fairly tall and thin with plenty of black hair. His teeth, which were irregular and widely spaced, stuck out a little even when he closed his mouth. As he spoke he took a printed form and a pencil from his pocket and he pulled up a chair and sat down.

"How are you feeling?"

There was no answer.

"Tough luck about your leg. I know how you feel. I hear you put up a fine show before they got you."

The man in the bed was lying quite still, watching the man in the chair.

The man in the chair said, "Well, let's get this stuff over. I'm afraid you'll have to answer a few questions so that I can fill in this combat report. Let me see now, first of all, what was your squadron?"

The man in the bed did not move. He looked straight at the Wing Commander and he said, "My name is Peter Williamson, my rank is Squadron Leader and my number is nine seven two four five seven."

My Lady Love, My Dove

It has been my habit for many years to take a nap after lunch. I settle myself in a chair in the living room with a cushion behind my head and my feet up on a small square leather stool, and I read until I drop off.

On this Friday afternoon, I was in my chair and feeling as comfortable as ever with a book in my hands—an old favorite, Doubleday and Westwood's *The Genera of Diurnal Lepidoptera*—when my wife, who has never been a silent lady, began to talk to me from the sofa opposite. "These two people," she said, "what time are they coming?"

I made no answer, so she repeated the question, louder this time. I told her politely that I didn't know.

"I don't think I like them very much." she said. "Especially him."

"No dear, all right."

"Arthur. I said I don't think I like them very much."

I lowered my book and looked across at her lying with her feet up on the sofa, flipping over the pages of some fashion magazine. "We've only met them once," I said.

"A dreadful man, really. Never stopped telling jokes, or stories, or something."

"I'm sure you'll manage them very well, dear."

"And she's pretty frightful, too. When do you think they'll arrive?"

Somewhere around six o'clock, I guessed.

"But don't *you* think they're awful?" she asked, pointing at me with her finger.

"Well . . ."

"They're *too* awful, they really are."

"We can hardly put them off now, Pamela."

"They're absolutely the end," she said.

"Then why did you ask them?" The question slipped out before I could stop myself and I regretted it at once, for it is a rule with me never to provoke my wife if I can help it. There was a pause, and I watched her face, waiting for the answer—the big white face that to me was something so strange and fascinating there were occasions when I could hardly bring myself to look away from it. In the evenings sometimes—working on her embroidery, or painting those small intricate flower pictures—the face would tighten and glimmer with a subtle inward strength that was beautiful beyond words, and I would sit and stare at it minute after minute while pretending to read. Even now, at this moment, with that compressed acid look, the frowning forehead, the petulant curl of the nose, I had to admit that there was a majestic quality about this woman, something splendid, almost stately; and so tall she was, far taller than I—although today, in her fifty-first year, I think one would have to call her big rather than tall.

"You know very well why I asked them," she answered sharply. "For bridge, that's all. They play an absolutely first-class game, and for a decent stake." She glanced up and saw me watching her. "Well," she said, "that's about the way you feel too, isn't it?"

"Well, of course, I . . ."

"Don't be a fool, Arthur."

"The only time I met them I must say they did seem quite nice."

"So is the butcher."

"Now Pamela, dear—please. We don't want any of that."

"Listen," she said, slapping down the magazine on her lap, "you saw the sort of people they were as well as I did. A pair of stupid climbers who think they can go anywhere just because they play good bridge."

"I'm sure you're right, dear, but what I don't honestly understand is why—"

"I keep telling you—so that for once we can get a decent game. I'm sick and tired of playing with rabbits. But I really can't see why I should have these awful people in the house."

"Of course not, my dear, but isn't it a little late now—"

"Arthur?"

"Yes?"

"Why for God's sake do you always argue with me? You *know* you disliked them as much as I did."

"I really don't think you need worry, Pamela. After all, they seemed quite a nice well-mannered young couple."

"Arthur, don't be pompous." She was looking at me hard with those wide gray eyes of hers, and to avoid them—they sometimes made me quite uncomfortable—I got up and walked over to the french windows that led into the garden.

The big sloping lawn out in front of the house was newly mown, striped with pale and dark ribbons of green. On the far side, the two laburnums were in full flower at last, the long golden chains making a blaze of color against the darker trees beyond. The roses were out too, and the scarlet begonias, and in the long herbaceous border all my lovely hybrid lupines, columbine, delphinium, sweet William, and the huge pale, scented iris. One of the gardeners was coming up the drive from his lunch. I could see the roof of his cottage through the trees, and beyond it to one side, the place where the drive went out through the iron gates on the Canterbury road.

My wife's house. Her garden. How beautiful it all was! How peaceful! Now, if only Pamela would try to be a little less solicitous of my welfare, less prone to coax me into doing things for my own good rather than for my own pleasure, then everything would be heaven. Mind you, I don't want to give the impression that I do not love her—I worship the very air she breathes—or that I can't manage her, or that I am not the captain of my ship. All I am trying to say is that she can be a trifle irritating at times, the way she carries on. For example, those little mannerisms of hers—I do wish she would drop them all, especially the way she has of pointing a finger at me to emphasize a phrase. You must remember that I am a man who is built rather small, and a gesture like this, when used to excess by a person like my wife, is apt to intimidate. I sometimes find it difficult to convince myself that she is not an overbearing woman.

"Arthur!" she called. "Come here."

"What?"

"I've just had a most marvelous idea. Come here."

I turned and went over to where she was lying on the sofa.

"Look," she said, "do you want to have some fun?"

"What sort of fun?"

"With the Snapes?"

"Who are the Snapes?"

"Come on," she said. "Wake up. Henry and Sally Snape. Our week-end guests."

"Well?"

"Now listen. I was lying here thinking how awful they really are . . . the way they behave . . . him with his jokes and her like a sort of love-crazed sparrow . . ." She hesitated, smiling slyly, and for some reason, I got the impression she was about to say a shocking thing. "Well—if that's the way they behave when they're in front of us, then what on earth must they be like when they're alone together?"

"Now wait a minute, Pamela—"

"Don't be an ass, Arthur. Let's have some fun—some real fun for once—tonight." She had half raised herself up off the sofa, her face bright with a kind of sudden recklessness, the mouth slightly open, and she was looking at me with two round gray eyes, a spark dancing slowly in each.

"Why shouldn't we?"

"What do you want to do?"

"Why, it's obvious. Can't you see?"

"No, I can't."

"All we've got to do is put a microphone in their room." I admit I was expecting something pretty bad, but when she said this I was so shocked I didn't know what to answer.

"That's exactly what we'll do," she said.

"Here!" I cried. "No. Wait a minute. You can't do that."

"Why not?"

"That's about the nastiest trick I ever heard of. It's like—why, it's like listening at keyholes, or reading letters, only far far worse. You don't mean this seriously, do you?"

"Of course I do."

I knew how much she disliked being contradicted, but there were times when I felt it necessary to assert myself, even at considerable risk. "Pamela," I said, snapping the words out, "I forbid you to do it!"

She took her feet down from the sofa and sat up straight. "What in God's name are you trying to pretend to be, Arthur? I simply don't understand you."

"That shouldn't be too difficult."

"Tommyrot! I've known you do lots of worse things than this before now."

"Never!"

"Oh yes I have. What makes you suddenly think you're a so much nicer person than I am?"

"I've never done things like that."

"All right, my boy," she said, pointing her finger at me like a pistol. "What about that time at the Milfords' last Christmas? Remember? You nearly laughed your head off and I had to put my hand over your mouth to stop them hearing us. What about that for one?"

"That was different," I said. "It wasn't our house. And they weren't our guests."

"It doesn't make any difference at all." She was sitting very upright, staring at me with those round gray eyes, and the chin was beginning to come up high in a peculiarly contemptuous manner. "Don't be such a pompous hypocrite," she said. "What on earth's come over you?"

"I really think it's a pretty nasty thing, you know, Pamela. I honestly do."

"But listen, Arthur. I'm a *nasty* person. And so are you—in a secret sort of way. That's why we get along together."

"I never heard such nonsense."

"Mind you, if you've suddenly decided to change your character completely, that's another story."

"You've got to stop talking this way, Pamela."

"You see," she said, "if you really *have* decided to reform, then what on earth am I going to do?"

"You don't know what you're saying."

"Arthur, how could a nice person like you want to associate with a stinker?"

I sat myself down slowly in the chair opposite her, and she was watching me all the time. You understand, she was a big woman, with a big white face, and when she looked at me hard, as she was doing now, I became—how shall I say it—surrounded, almost enveloped by her, as though she were a great tub of cream and I had fallen in.

"You don't honestly want to do this microphone thing, do you?"

"But of course I do. It's time we had a bit of fun around here. Come on, Arthur. Don't be so stuffy."

"It's not right, Pamela."

"It's just as right"—up came the finger again—"just as right as when you found those letters of Mary Probert's in her purse and you read them through from beginning to end."

"We should never have done that."

"*We!*"

"You read them afterwards, Pamela."

"It didn't harm anyone at all. You said so yourself at the time. And this one's no worse."

"How would *you* like it if someone did it to *you?*"

"How could I *mind* if I didn't know it was being done? Come on, Arthur. Don't be so flabby."

"I'll have to think about it."

"Maybe the great radio engineer doesn't know how to connect the mike to the speaker?"

"That's the easiest part."

"Well, go on then. Go on and do it."

"I'll think about it and let you know later."

"There's no time for that. They might arrive any moment."

"Then I won't do it. I'm not going to be caught red-handed."

"If they come before you're through, I'll simply keep them down here. No danger. What's the time, anyway?"

It was nearly three o'clock.

"They're driving down from London," she said, "and they certainly won't leave till after lunch. That gives you plenty of time."

"Which room are you putting them in?"

"The big yellow room at the end of the corridor. That's not too far away, is it?"

"I suppose it could be done."

"And by the by," she said, "where are you going to have the speaker?"

"I haven't said I'm going to do it yet."

"My God!" she cried, "I'd like to see someone try and stop you now. You ought to see your face. It's all pink and excited at the very prospect. Put the speaker in our bedroom why not? But go on—and hurry."

I hesitated. It was something I made a point of doing whenever she tried to order me about, instead of asking nicely. "I don't like it, Pamela."

She didn't say any more after that; she just sat there, absolutely still, watching me, a resigned, waiting expression on her face, as though she were in a long queue. This, I knew from experience, was a danger signal. She was like one of those bomb things with the pin pulled out, and it was only a matter of time before—bang! and she would explode. In the silence that followed, I could almost hear her ticking.

So I got up quietly and went out to the workshop and collected a mike and a hundred and fifty feet of wire. Now that I was away from her, I am ashamed to admit that I began to feel a bit of excitement myself, a tiny warm prickling sensation under the skin, near the tips of my fingers. It was nothing much, mind you—really nothing at all. Good heavens, I experience the same thing every morning of my life when I open the paper to check the closing prices on two or three of my wife's larger stockholdings. So I wasn't going to get carried away by a silly joke like this. At the same time, I couldn't help being amused.

I took the stairs two at a time and entered the yellow room at the end of the passage. It had the clean, unlived-in appearance of all guest rooms, with its twin beds, yellow satin bedspreads, pale yellow walls, and golden-colored curtains. I began to look around for a good place to hide the mike. This was the most important part of all, for whatever happened, it must not be discovered. I thought first of the basket of logs by the fireplace. Put it under the logs. No—not safe enough. Behind the radiator? On top of the wardrobe? Under the desk? None of these seemed very professional to me. All might be subject to chance inspection because of a dropped collar stud or something like that. Finally, with considerable cunning, I decided to put it inside the springing of the sofa. The sofa was against the wall, near the edge of the carpet, and my lead wire could go straight under the carpet over to the door.

I tipped up the sofa and slit the material underneath. Then I tied the microphone securely up among the springs, making sure that it faced the room. After that, I led the wire under the carpet to the door.

I was calm and cautious in everything I did. Where the wire had to emerge from under the carpet and pass out of the door, I made a little groove in the wood so that it was almost invisible.

All this, of course, took time, and when I suddenly heard the crunch of wheels on the gravel of the drive outside, and then the slamming of car doors and the voices of our guests, I was still only halfway down the corridor, tacking the wire along the skirting. I stopped and straightened up, hammer in hand, and I must confess that I felt afraid. You have no idea how unnerving that noise was to me. I experienced the same sudden stomachy feeling of fright as when a bomb once dropped the other side of the village during the war, one afternoon, while I was working quietly in the library with my butterflies.

Don't worry, I told myself. Pamela will take care of these people. She won't let them come up here.

Rather frantically, I set about finishing the job, and soon I had the wire tacked all along the corridor and through into our bedroom. Here, concealment was not so important, although I still did not permit myself to get careless because of the servants. So I laid the wire under the carpet and brought it up unobtrusively into the back of the radio. Making the final connections was an elementary technical matter and took me no time at all.

Well—I had done it. I stepped back and glanced at the little radio. Somehow, now, it looked different—no longer a silly box for making noises but an evil little creature that crouched on the tabletop with a part of its own body reaching out secretly into a forbidden place far away. I switched it on. It hummed faintly but made no other sound. I took my bedside clock, which had a loud tick, and carried it along to the yellow room and placed it on the floor by the sofa. When I returned, sure enough the radio creature was ticking away as loudly as if the clock were in the room—even louder.

I fetched back the clock. Then I tidied myself up in the bathroom, returned my tools to the workshop, and prepared to meet the guests. But first, to compose myself, and so that I would not have to appear in front of them with the blood, as it were, still wet on my hands, I spent five minutes in the library with my collection. I concentrated on a tray of the lovely *Vanessa cardui*—the "painted lady"—and made a few notes for a paper I was preparing entitled "The Relation between Color Pattern and Framework of Wings," which I intended to read at the next meeting of our society in Canterbury. In this way I soon regained my normal grave, attentive manner.

When I entered the living room, our two guests, whose names I could never remember, were seated on the sofa. My wife was mixing drinks.

"Oh, *there* you are, Arthur," she said. "Where *have* you been?"

I thought this was an unnecessary remark. "I'm so sorry," I said to the guests as we shook hands. "I was busy and forgot the time."

"We all know what *you've* been doing," the girl said, smiling wisely. "But we'll forgive him, won't we, dearest?"

"I think we should," the husband answered.

I had a frightful, fantastic vision of my wife telling them, amidst roars of laughter, precisely what I had been doing upstairs. She *couldn't*— she *couldn't* have done that! I looked round at her and she too was smiling as she measured out the gin.

"I'm sorry we disturbed you," the girl said.

I decided that if this was going to be a joke then I'd better join in quickly, so I forced myself to smile with her.

"You must let us see it," the girl continued.

"See what?"

"Your collection. Your wife says that they are absolutely beautiful."

I lowered myself slowly into a chair and relaxed. It was ridiculous to be so nervous and jumpy. "Are you interested in butterflies?" I asked her.

"I'd love to see yours, Mr. Beauchamp."

The martinis were distributed and we settled down to a couple of hours of talk and drink before dinner. It was from then on that I began to form the impression that our guests were a charming couple. My wife, coming from a titled family, is apt to be conscious of her class and breeding, and is often hasty in her judgment of strangers who are friendly towards her—particularly tall men. She is frequently right, but in this case I felt that she might be making a mistake. As a rule, I myself do not like tall men either; they are apt to be supercilious and omniscient. But Henry Snape—my wife had whispered his name—struck me as being an amiable simple young man with good manners whose main preoccupation, very properly, was Mrs. Snape. He was handsome in a long-faced, horsy sort of way, with dark-brown eyes that seemed to be gentle and sympathetic. I envied him his fine mop of black hair, and caught myself wondering what lotion he used to keep it looking so healthy. He did tell us one or two jokes, but they were on a high level and no one could have objected.

"At school," he said, "they used to call me Scervix. Do you know why?"

"I haven't the least idea," my wife answered.

"Because cervix is Latin for nape."

This was rather deep and it took me a while to work out.

"What school was that, Mr. Snape?" my wife asked.

"Eton," he said, and my wife gave a quick little nod of approval. Now she will talk to him, I thought, so I turned my attention to the other one, Sally Snape. She was an attractive girl with a bosom. Had I met her fifteen years earlier I might well have got myself into some sort of trouble. As it was, I had a pleasant enough time telling her all about my beautiful butterflies. I was observing her closely as I talked, and after a while I began to get the impression that she was not, in fact, quite so merry and smiling a girl as I had been led to believe at first. She seemed to be coiled in herself, as though with a secret she was jealously guarding. The deep blue eyes moved too quickly about the room, never settling or resting on one thing for more than a moment; and over all her face, though so faint that they might not even have been there, those small downward lines of sorrow.

"I'm so looking forward to our game of bridge," I said, finally changing the subject.

"Us too," she answered. "You know we play almost every night, we love it so."

"You are extremely expert, both of you. How did you get to be so good?"

"It's practice," she said. "That's all. Practice, practice, practice."

"Have you played in any championships?"

"Not yet, but Henry wants very much for us to do that. It's hard work, you know, to reach that standard. Terribly hard work." Was there not here, I wondered, a hint of resignation in her voice? Yes, that was probably it; he was pushing her too hard, making her take it too seriously, and the poor girl was tired of it all.

At eight o'clock, without changing, we moved in to dinner. The meal went well, with Henry Snape telling us some very droll stories. He also praised my Richebourg '34 in a most knowledgeable fashion, which pleased me greatly. By the time coffee came, I realized that I had grown to like these two youngsters immensely, and as a result I began to feel uncomfortable about this microphone business. It would have been all right if they had been horrid people, but to play this trick on two such charming young persons as these filled me with a strong sense of guilt. Don't misunderstand me. I was not getting cold feet. It didn't seem necessary to stop the operation. But I refused to relish the prospect openly as my wife seemed now to be doing, with covert smiles and winks and secret little noddings of the head.

Around nine-thirty, feeling comfortable and well fed, we returned to the large living room to start our bridge. We were playing for a fair stake—ten shillings a hundred—so we decided not to split families, and I partnered my wife the whole time. We all four of us took the game seriously, which is the only way to take it, and we played silently, intently, hardly speaking at all except to bid. It was not the money we played for. Heaven knows, my wife had enough of that, and so apparently did the Snapes. But among experts it is almost traditional that they play for a reasonable stake.

That night the cards were evenly divided, but for once my wife played badly, so we got the worst of it. I could see that she wasn't concentrating fully, and as we came along towards midnight she began not even to care. She kept glancing up at me with those large gray eyes of hers, the eyebrows raised, the nostrils curiously open, a little gloating smile around the corner of her mouth.

Our opponents played a fine game. Their bidding was masterly, and all through the evening they made only one mistake. That was when the girl badly overestimated her partner's hand and bid six spades. I doubled and they went three down, vulnerable, which cost them eight hundred points. It was just a momentary lapse, but I remember that Sally Snape was very put out by it, even though her husband forgave her at once, kissing her hand across the table and telling her not to worry.

Around twelve-thirty my wife announced that she wanted to go to bed.

"Just one more rubber?" Henry Snape said.

"No, Mr. Snape. I'm tired tonight. Arthur's tired, too. I can see it. Let's all go to bed."

She herded us out of the room and we went upstairs, the four of us together. On the way up, there was the usual talk about breakfast and what they wanted and how they were to call the maid. "I think you'll like your room," my wife said. "It has a view right across the valley, and the sun comes to you in the morning around ten o'clock."

We were in the passage now, standing outside our own bedroom door, and I could see the wire I had put down that afternoon and how it ran along the top of the skirting down to their room. Although it was nearly the same color as the paint, it looked very conspicuous to me. "Sleep well," my wife said. "Sleep well, Mrs. Snape. Good night, Mr. Snape." I followed her into our room and shut the door.

"Quick!" she cried. "Turn it on!" My wife was always like that, frightened that she was going to miss something. She had a reputation, when she went hunting—I never go myself—of always being right up with the hounds whatever the cost to herself or her horse for fear that that she might miss a kill. I could see she had no intention of missing this one.

The little radio warmed up just in time to catch the noise of their door opening and closing again.

"There!" my wife said. "They've gone in." She was standing in the center of the room in her blue dress, her hands clasped before her, her head craned forward, intently listening, and the whole of the big white face seemed somehow to have gathered itself together, tight like a wineskin.

Almost at once the voice of Henry Snape came out of the radio, strong and clear. "You're just a goddam little fool," he was saying, and this voice was so different from the one I remembered, so harsh and unpleasant, it made me jump. "The whole bloody evening wasted! Eight hundred points—that's eight pounds between us!"

"I got mixed up," the girl answered. "I won't do it again, I promise."

"What's *this*?" my wife said. "What's going on?" Her mouth was wide open now, the eyebrows stretched up high, and she came quickly over to the radio and leaned forward, ear to the speaker. I must say I felt rather excited myself.

"I promise, I promise I won't do it again," the girl was saying.

"We're not taking any chances," the man answered grimly. "We're going to have another practice right now."

"Oh no, please! I couldn't stand it!"

"Look," the man said, "all the way out here to take money off this rich bitch and you have to go and mess it up."

My wife's turn to jump.

"The second time this week," he went on.

"I promise I won't do it again."

"Sit down. I'll sing them out and you answer."

"No, Henry, *please*! Not all five hundred of them. It'll take three hours."

"All right, then. We'll leave out the finger positions. I think you're sure of those. We'll just do the basic bids showing honor tricks."

"Oh, Henry, must we? I'm so tired."

"It's absolutely essential that you get them perfect," he said. "We have a game every day next week, you know that. And we've got to eat."

"What is this?" my wife whispered. "What on earth is it?"

"Shhh!" I said. "Listen!"

"All right," the man's voice was saying. "Now we'll start from the beginning. Ready?"

"Oh Henry, *please*!" She sounded very near to tears.

"Come on, Sally. Pull yourself together."

Then, in a quite different voice, the one we had been used to hearing in the living room, Henry Snape said, "*One* club." I noticed that there was a curious lilting emphasis on the word "one," the first part of the word drawn out long.

"Ace queen of clubs," the girl replied wearily. "King jack of spades. No hearts, and ace jack of diamonds."

"And how many cards to each suit? Watch my finger positions carefully."

"You said we could miss those."

"Well—if you're quite sure you know them?"

"Yes, I know them."

A pause, then, "A *club*."

"King jack of clubs," the girl recited. "Ace of spades. Queen jack of hearts, and ace queen of diamonds."

Another pause, then "I'll say *one* club."

"Ace king of clubs . . ."

"My heavens alive!" I cried. "It's a bidding code! They show every card in the hand!"

"Arthur, it couldn't be!"

"It's like those men who go into the audience and borrow something from you and there's a girl blindfolded on the stage, and from the way he phrases the question she can tell him exactly what it is—even a railway ticket, and what station it's from."

"It's impossible!"

"Not at all. But it's tremendous hard work to learn. Listen to them."

"I'll go *one heart,*" the man's voice was saying.

"King queen ten of hearts. Ace jack of spades. No diamonds. Queen jack of clubs . . ."

"And you see," I said, "he tells her the *number* of cards he has in each suit by the position of his fingers."

"How?"

"I don't know. You heard him saying about it."

"My *God,* Arthur! Are you sure that's what they're doing?"

"I'm afraid so." I watched her as she walked quickly over to the side of the bed to fetch a cigarette. She lit it with her back to me and then swung round, blowing the smoke up at the ceiling in a thin stream. I knew we were going to have to do something about this, but I wasn't quite sure what because we couldn't possibly accuse them without revealing the source of our information. I waited for my wife's decision.

"Why, Arthur," she said slowly, blowing out clouds of smoke. "Why, this is a *mar-velous* idea. D'you think *we* could learn to do it?"

"What!"

"Of course. Why not?"

"Here! No! Wait a minute, Pamela . . ." but she came swiftly across the room, right up close to me where I was standing, and she dropped her head and looked down at me—the old look of a smile that wasn't a smile, at the corners of the mouth, and the curl of the nose, and the big full gray eyes staring at me with their bright black centers, and then they were gray, and all the rest was white flecked with hundreds of tiny red veins—and when she looked at me like this, hard and close, I swear to you it made me feel as though I were drowning.

"Yes," she said. "Why not?"

"But Pamela . . . Good heavens . . . No . . . After all . . ."

"Arthur, I do wish you wouldn't *argue* with me all the time. That's exactly what we'll do. Now, go fetch a deck of cards; we'll start right away."